YOUR ONE
A HENDERSON FAMILY SPIN-OFF NOVEL

MONICA WALTERS

CONTENTS

INTRODUCTION

Hello, readers!

Thank you for purchasing and/or downloading this book. This work of art contains *explicit language, moments of depression,* and *lewd sex scenes.* This book is an insta-love story, as most of my books tend to be. If any of the previously mentioned offend you or serve as triggers for unpleasant times, please do NOT read.

This is a **Henderson Family Saga** spin-off novel. There are some issues that are spoken of in this book that happened in previous books, mainly in *A Country Hood Christmas with the Hendersons, Where Is The Love, Don't Walk Away,* and *Healing For My Soul* that I don't go into great detail about. It's in your best interest to read them in this order, though, because you won't understand by only picking up those four. Here's the list:

The Country Hood Love Stories
8 Seconds to Love- Legend and Harper
Breaking Barriers to Your Heart- Red and Shana

Training My Heart to Love You- Zayson and Kortlynn

This book also contains characters from my **Written Between the Pages Series**. *The Devil Goes to Church Too* gives background information on Nate's biological father, David Guillory, and his relationship with Raquel and Noah. Book two, *The Book of Noah*, gives details as to how David died. *The Revelations of Ryan Jr.* is book three, but there is no pertinent info there. Finally, book four, *The Rebirth of Noah*, details the relationship between Noah and TAZ.

While it isn't necessary to read this series to understand what's going on, again, it will give you the background information that I don't go into great detail about.

Also, please remember that your reality isn't everyone's reality. What may seem unrealistic to you could be very real for someone else. But also keep in mind that, despite the previous statement, this is a fictional story.

If you are okay with the previously mentioned warnings, I hope that you enjoy the story of Nate Guillory and Kenya Zenith.

Monica

P.S.- TAZ and Taryn are the same person. Kenya typically refers to her sister as Taryn, and Nate calls her TAZ (her stage name).

PROLOGUE
NATE

When I got to my mother's house, I could feel my irritation heighten. This conversation was long overdue, and it was partially my fault why it hadn't been had yet. I was way too angry to talk to her about it, after I'd learned more about my deceased father. Although the man she told me was my father had died years ago, she didn't tell me he was my father until after his death. She should have just kept that shit to herself at that point.

It wasn't like I could establish a relationship with him. Knowing he was my dad, wasn't for my benefit though. I realized years later what it was all about. She needed me to benefit from him financially. I remembered going to do bloodwork when I was fifteen or so. I now knew that was to prove he was my father. As my legal guardian, she had a right to some of David's money.

David Guillory was an amazing basketball player, and I enjoyed watching him play for the Wizards later in his career, as a kid, not knowing I could have been watching live and in living color. I didn't notice how much we resembled until I knew of our connection. David had even more of a spotlight on him because of his connection to the famous rapper Noah. He was his stepfather at some point and had been a part of his life since he was four years old.

I only reached out to Noah six months ago, because now that I was a famous basketball player, I knew he would take me seriously and wouldn't be as hesitant to meet me. Since our acquaintance, I knew he probably would have met with me regardless, whether I was famous or not. He was just that great of a guy. Listening to all his stories of how great a father figure David had been for him infuriated me.

My mother had denied me the opportunity to know my father, a man that could have had so much influence over my life. Years after she told me he was my dad, she said she wasn't sure at the time of her pregnancy if he was indeed my father. The older I got, the more I started to look like him. Plus, I'd had a growth spurt the summer before tenth grade and grew damn near a foot taller. That was when she knew for sure. However, that was during our second talk about him. The first talk when I was a kid was that he was a horrible person… a womanizer that wouldn't have been a good father to me.

Apparently, she was a player, too, if she didn't know who my father was, unless what she said in the second vital conversation was a lie. I believed she needed a more concrete excuse as to why she didn't tell me about him or him about me. Just the statement that she didn't think he would be a good father was fickle as hell, but it got her by when I was fifteen. That shit didn't fly after I was grown.

I opened the door as I took a deep breath and got out of the car. Making my way to her front door, it seemed my steps got heavier and heavier. I really didn't want to rehash this shit again with her, but in order for us to move on, I knew I had to. She'd noticed my distance since I'd met Noah, and I knew that she was probably aware that I'd learned more about David that caused me to back away for a minute.

Noah didn't just tell me about how great of a person David was. He also told me about his struggles with his mother as her husband. Who

David was to him didn't waver though. He never mistreated Noah, and I knew there were certain issues about Noah's birth father between Noah's mother and him that made shit difficult. That was probably why he couldn't maintain any relationships after her. She was the woman he truly loved.

Noah didn't find out who his birth father was until he was almost thirty. The difference between him and me was that he'd known his father all along and had a healthy relationship with him his entire life. He just didn't know that was his father. Although there was a brief rift after the revelation, they were able to move on from it and establish an even stronger bond, especially now that his father was now his mother's husband and had been for fifteen years.

Before I could knock, the door opened. My mom gave me a weak smile. "Congratulations on the win, baby," she said as she stepped aside to let me in.

"Thanks, Ma," I said, then kissed her cheek.

Sheila Green was a good mother to me. This was the only issue we'd ever had. It just happened to be a major issue that couldn't be overlooked. She had plenty of help from my grandparents when I was younger, and I didn't want for anything. She provided a good life for me, putting hers on hold to see to that.

This issue was weighing heavily on me though. I was grateful for the life she provided, but I would never know how the love from my father would have felt. While I knew I had to move on from this, I also knew the only way I could do that was to expose my true feelings to her.

After she closed the door, she joined me on the couch in the front room in silence. When she grabbed my hand and rubbed it between hers, it eased my irritation, and I was grateful for that. As I struggled to begin, she said, "Just tell me you aren't kicking me out of your life."

I frowned slightly as I stared at her. "Why would you think I would do that?"

"I can feel your anger."

"I'm not angry anymore, but I can admit that I'm irritated. Listening to Noah talk about how David stepped up to be a father to him, despite his difficulties with his mother, lets me know that you caused me to miss out on someone great because you couldn't get past yourself. You denied me a relationship with him, either because you were angry at him or you were embarrassed, and now, I can never have one. I'm left here wondering how my life would have been different had he been a part of it."

She pulled her hand away and met my gaze. "So you think you would have been better off by having a relationship with him?"

"I didn't say that. Do you think that?" I challenged.

She stood from her seat and paced. "I did what I thought was best, and now I'm getting crucified for it?"

"No one's crucifying you. The fact that you're getting so defensive about it lets me know there's more that you haven't told me. My voice hasn't wavered, so please don't elevate yours. I haven't been disrespectful, so this conversation doesn't warrant that. I'm trying to get an understanding of things and express how I feel about it as a grown man after my enlightenment on who David Guillory was as a father, not just an individual."

"What understanding do you need? We've had this conversation twice, Nate."

"And each time, I've gotten a different response."

I stood as she continued to pace. My face adorned a slight frown, which I was sure portrayed my confusion with her sudden attitude change. It seemed she was prepared for the conversation at first, and now she was defensive and nervous. I slid my hand down my face as I took a deep breath.

"Mama, I'm trying to get you to understand how I feel about this. Since talking to Noah, I've been trying to figure out a way to approach you about it. This is the calmest I've been about it, but now you're giving me a violent, emotional shove back into being angry. Is it wrong for me to feel like I missed out on someone great... someone who could have greatly impacted my life as well? I feel like you didn't think about me and what was best for me at all. Your decisions were about you."

"Get out, Nate. I can't deal with this right now."

"See what I'm saying? All I really expected of you, today, was for you to listen, maybe sympathize with how I was feeling, and offer words of comfort. Although a long shot, I was even hoping you would apologize for how your decision affected me. You're making this situation a lot worse than what it has to be. It didn't have to be like this. We could have sat here like adults and just talked. It ain't like you can change any of this shit."

"I said, get out! Now!"

I nodded repeatedly, accepting where our relationship was headed, and pulled my car remote from my pocket. Giving her one last look of disgust and disappointment, I turned and headed to the door. When I got to it, I realized what was happening. She was forcing me out of her life, for whatever reason, since I didn't come here to tell her I was done with her. I just didn't know why. Jessica Monroe was wrong. This talk and me trying to understand her didn't help.

Until Sheila was ready to move past whatever was hindering her, we would be stuck in this rut. I'd done what I thought I needed to do for me. Unfortunately, my mama had done the same, and I had to live with that.

CHAPTER 1

NATE

THREE MONTHS LATER...

Y*ou still can't be in her presence without approaching her, huh?*

I glanced at Jakari's text message as I chilled out on the couch at home. Noah was on tour and had made his way back to Houston. Although it was the end of March and the season was still in full swing, my next game was a home game. I turned down his invitation because I knew Jess would be there. I felt like a fucking punk about it too.

I can be in her presence without approaching her. I can't be in her presence without getting sick from all those curves I should be gracing in front of her man. How is she?

I rolled my eyes and threw my phone to the coffee table in front of me. I knew how she was doing. While I hadn't reached out since her message about letting go, I followed her on Instagram. She'd posted her maternity pictures a couple of days ago, and she looked like she was ready to drop that baby any minute. Unfortunately, I felt like I was clinging to Jessica, not only because I loved her and we had an intense connection, but because I felt like I was missing something.

Ever since that last discussion with my mom right after Christmas, things had been different in my life. She told me I owed her an apology. Well, the way my personality was set up, I was honest to a fault. I wasn't going to apologize if I hadn't done shit. I wasn't going to be the bigger person for her. She was gonna have to see that I wasn't folding on that subject. While I had gotten past the fact that she kept me from him, I wasn't past her response from three months ago.

My phone chimed, and I was sure it was a message from Jakari, but then it rang. I grabbed it to see a FaceTime call from TAZ. I couldn't answer. I knew she wanted me to feel a part of the moment without being a part of the moment. If I wasn't there in person, I didn't want to see what I was missing out on. If I would have had a game or a prior engagement, that would have been different.

Clicking on the text from Jakari, I read, *She's cool. Her due date is in like two weeks. She probably shouldn't even be here, but you know nobody can tell Jessica shit. LOL*

Boy, did I know it. I swore she was my one when I met her a little over a year ago. Now that I'd introduced her to Noah, I couldn't even fucking function in my element without possibly running into her. Lennox was one of my best friends that I couldn't drop in and see freely, and because of my involvement with her, my presence was frowned upon, like I didn't know Lennox first. It left me on the outside of things.

She said Brixton was somewhat insecure because he could see how much I loved her, but I wanted to believe that he could see how much she felt for me as well. That was the shit that really had him tight. I couldn't understand how she even chose him over me after what we shared. I supposed that shit wasn't as strong for her as it was for me. Maybe what she gave me was a sympathy fuck.

Whatever it was, it had me fiending. I didn't like that feeling. If she were mine, it would be different. I would be her sucker all damn day. To be a sucker for a woman that wasn't mine was frustrating. I'd gone out on a date with a woman I met that was working for Golden State, but I didn't feel shit spark. She was a nice woman, but it felt like a waste of three hours for me.

I didn't too much care for hanging with my teammates, because most of them were younger than me and on bullshit. I had always been an old soul. Noah and I had that in common. I wasn't with the party scene or fucking around. I bonded with my older teammates, but most of them had families or had retired. This was a different situation I found myself in. I was a loner.

Although I was an only child, I was never a true loner. I usually had family to hang around or close friends. My mama wasn't speaking to me, and all my closest friends were close to her. I didn't know what to do with my fucking self. Instead of sitting here moping, I decided to go ahead and get ready to head back to Dallas. *I should be at that fucking concert.*

At least if I left now, I wouldn't have to drive on game day. It was a three-and-a-half-hour drive, and I could be at my Dallas home before midnight. After grabbing a couple of bottles of alkaline water, I went to my Range. It was rare I stayed at the house in Dallas when I didn't have a game there, because I didn't have anyone close to me there, but it seemed I was getting the same vibes in H-Town.

Once I was in the driver's seat, I pulled up my thread with Jakari and replied. *Glad she's well. I'm about to head to Dallas tonight. Holla later.*

Jakari was Jess's cousin and the only one that pretty much stayed cool with me. I talked to him more than I talked to Lennox these days. I understood he was busy with their new baby, though; not to mention, he was a newlywed. I still needed someone to know I was on the move. I always liked for someone to know my whereabouts. I supposed it was old school of me.

My mama and grandparents always wanted to know where I was, just in case they needed to get to me. That practice had become habit and stayed with me. Before I could back out the driveway, he messaged back. *Be careful. I'll holla when I can.*

He had a baby on the way as well and was entertaining a new relationship. Everyone close to me seemed to be progressing in life, and my issues and mental state had mine at a fucking standstill. While Jess was important to me, I knew it was this situation with my mama that had me depressed.

In three months, I hadn't had a decent conversation with her. We only talked when I called her or when I texted her. I never realized just how stubborn she was until now. I talked to my grandparents, and they agreed that I owed her an apology because it was something she'd already addressed, regardless that she gave me two different explanations. She was my mother and did what was right by me. So, needless to say, my stance on this situation had alienated me from everyone.

As I drove, my phone chimed, but I knew it was a message on Instagram. I got those quite often. I wasn't in a hurry to check it. People tagged me in shit all the time. Usually, it was rumors about me or someone I was connected to. I couldn't understand why people were so interested in celebrities' personal lives. I never got off into that. I admired basketball players and was a true fan of quite a few of them, but I didn't know much about their personal lives. Frankly, I didn't care.

My curiosity got the best of me after a few miles, probably because I didn't have shit else to do, and I saw a direct message from 'the country hood princess'. I felt hot all of a sudden. Why in the fuck was she messaging me? She said we shouldn't speak anymore. Jess was fucking with me, and I couldn't hang around for that shit. I was geared up to tell her a piece of my mind in that message until I saw what she had to say.

I'm so sorry. I overheard TAZ say that you were invited to the

concert. I know why you aren't here. I'll do my best to be more consid-
erate of you since we share the same people now. Noah is like your
brother, and you introduced me to him. I should have fallen back on
this one. I hope you are well.

I set my phone back in the compartment under the radio without
responding. If I said anything to her, I wouldn't be able to stop talking
to her. Her aura made me a weak ass nigga, and I'd be damned. I
grabbed my phone again and felt the pain in my chest as I blocked her
profile. This whole thing was toxic.

She considered me a friend, but I considered her as everything but
that. She said she would stop reaching out, so now I had to make sure
she couldn't. I respected her decisions, so I had to make sure she
started respecting her decisions too.

"DAMN, I WISH YOU COULD HAVE BEEN AT THE CONCERT. I PERFORM IN
Miami next week. Can you make that one?"

"Most likely. We play Miami next Saturday."

"Shit! That's what's up! The concert is Friday. I hope you can fall
through."

I didn't understand why Noah wanted me at the concert so bad. I
slightly rolled my eyes and slowly shook my head. "Why? What's up?"

"I have something planned. Don't worry about what. You'll see
when you get there."

I wasn't even excited. Surprises never usually worked out in my
favor. It had been a week since I missed the concert in Houston, and I
was chilling at his house for his baby girl's first birthday party. She
was a beautiful little, brown-skinned princess that they'd named
Brooklyn. She looked just like Noah and his oldest daughter, Noelle.

He set her on my lap, and she quickly slid off to follow him. "Da-
Da!"

"Brook, I need you to stay with Uncle Nate, baby."

I picked her up as I shook my head. The doorbell rang, so he left to answer it. The past week had been uneventful. I had spent a lot of time in the gym, and as Noah suggested, I had been praying a lot and reading devotionals. I was trying to be at peace within, but it was hard as hell. I'd reached out to my mama and told her that I missed her. Her absence in my life was killing me slowly. It had always been me and her.

She'd responded that she missed me too and that she loved me. That was the highlight of my week. Maybe she would eventually come around, and we could talk yet again. Noah returned with TAZ's sister, Kenya. I set Brooklyn on her feet and stood from my seat as she smiled and said, "There's my favorite basketball player!"

I smiled back as I leaned over to hug her. I was probably a foot and a half taller than her. I got that shit often though. Being that I was six feet ten inches, I knew I would never find a woman my height. I could probably get close if I ventured to the WNBA games. "What's up, Kenya?"

"Not too much. Good game last night."

"We lost."

"What that got to do with your individual performance?"

"I don't even look at my stats when we lose. My contribution meant nothing if the team failed to convert it to a win."

She released me and gave me a smile. "Well, you had eighteen points, four assists, and a block. I love a team player. Never lose sight of that."

She winked at me. When she walked away, I couldn't help but scan her figure as I sat. I always thought she was a beautiful woman... since my first time meeting her. Her ass was off-limits too, though. She had a man that I was sure would be here later. When I asked Noah about her a couple of months ago, he informed me of her relationship status. I had yet to meet her man, but I could count on one hand how many times I'd even been around her.

Most times I saw Noah, we were in a city away from where she would be. She lived in Chicago, but Noah and TAZ lived in Baltimore. The first time I met her was here in Baltimore. She was here visiting TAZ for a couple of days. Then I saw her again at a concert in Los Angeles. Both times, she looked amazing, but I couldn't fully focus on that shit, because I was stuck up Jessica's ass.

"I saw that."

I glanced over at Noah. "Saw what?"

He twisted his lips to the side as the doorbell rang again. "You can act like you don't know what I'm talking about if you want to."

He walked away as I rolled my eyes. He paid attention too damn much. Just because I was admiring her didn't mean I was going to break up her happy home. I refused to be a homewrecker. That was why I blocked Jessica's country hood ass. When he came back and he had my mama in tow, I stood, the shock evident on my face, I was sure.

My eyes had widened significantly. She walked over to me and immediately hugged me tightly as Noah smiled. "Ma... how did you know I was here? I mean, what are you doing here?"

She pulled away, put her hand to my cheek, and said, "Hey, baby. I'm so sorry. Let's talk. I don't want this to be an ongoing issue. It has gone on long enough. Noah reached out, and I nearly crumbled when he started praying for me."

"Nate, y'all go to the studio so you can have privacy. You know the access code."

I nodded as I heard his brother's voice boom throughout the house. RJ's deep voice could have had all the pictures falling off the walls. I grabbed my mama's hand and led her down the long hallway. I glanced back at her, feeling whole again, and we hadn't even talked yet. She smiled and squeezed my hand.

After entering the code and opening the door, she walked in and sat on the couch. I sat next to her and grabbed her hand again. I was liter-ally in shock. While I was optimistic about us eventually repairing our relationship, I didn't expect her to show up here.

"I knew this was the last place you would expect me to show up. I wanted to surprise you. Noah is a good man, and he helped me to realize how I was tearing down the good man I'd raised because of my pride. You deserve the whole truth, no matter how embarrassing it is."

"You have nothing to be embarrassed about. You aren't the same woman you were back then, over thirty years ago. Nor are you the same woman you were months ago. I don't hold grudges. You know that."

I could be angry for a while, but after a sufficient amount of time had passed, my body naturally cleansed itself of whatever I was harboring. I loved my mama, and not having a relationship with her anymore had me dying inside. I was happy that she took the initiative to make this right.

She nodded and gently pulled her hand away from mine. "I'm just gonna start from the beginning. David and I went to high school together, so we were familiar. He wasn't just a stranger I met. However, James was a stranger."

Who in the fuck is James?

A confused frown made its way to my brow, but I didn't say a word. I knew she would reveal the answers to all my silent questions. "David and I had reconnected when he came home to visit. I saw him at a benefit for muscular dystrophy that one of our classmates was spearheading. We exchanged numbers and promised to catch up. We did. We talked on the phone often. I knew all about his relationship with Raquel and how they didn't work out because of his philandering ways. He'd allowed the limelight to consume him."

I remembered Noah talking about how he was eight or so when his mom and David broke up the first time. My mom fidgeted as she strug-gled to continue. The truth had been plaguing her. I could tell that much with how difficult this was for her. Revealing her flaws, especially to me, probably made her feel like I would think less of her. She was so uncomfortable.

"We maintained contact by phone, and whenever he came home to visit, we'd go out. Well, by his second or third visit, we crossed into uncharted territory. While I thought things were progressing to something special between us, neither of us had made a commitment to the other. While he was gone, I went out on a date with someone else. James was a stranger to me, but he was also a ball player. He played for Houston. We had sex, and within a month of that, David confronted me about it."

Oh shit. She'd hurt him. However, if what she was telling me was true, she didn't need to be embarrassed about that. If they hadn't established boundaries and desires, then she wasn't a mind reader.

"He told me that he'd planned to make me his when he came back to town. He said I'd given him hope that there was a woman that he could feel as deeply for as he felt for Raquel, Noah's mom, but I'd proved him wrong. That I'd used him. He thought I felt as strongly for him as he did for me. I argued that I felt like he didn't want a future with me and threw his reputation in his face, and that only hardened his heart more."

She swiped the tear from her cheek. "Truth was, I wasn't built for the distance. I felt like he was falling for me. Although he never said so until that moment, I felt it in every phone conversation. We reconnected at a time when he was vulnerable and wanting a love like the one he'd lost years before. I hurt him. Turned out, James had went running his mouth because he didn't like David, telling him that he'd fucked his woman. David waited a couple of weeks before even saying something to me about it. I knew it was because he didn't want to disrespect me."

I closed my eyes and slid my arm around her. *Damn.* "I'm sorry, Ma. That had to be tough."

"It was, but it was my own fault for not being honest with David. I could feel where we were heading. I should have put a stop to it. Three weeks after that, I found out I was pregnant. In my heart, I felt like you were David's, but I didn't want him to think I was trying to trap him. Plus, I knew he would blast my business about me fucking with James and insisting we got a DNA test, so I didn't say anything to either of them."

I kissed her head as the tears rained down her cheeks. This shit had been torturing her for years. I could understand why she didn't tell me this story when she first told me David was my father. I wasn't mature enough to handle the truth. I was only fifteen. "Mama, it's okay. I totally understand. I wish you would have told me years ago so we didn't have to go through that painful argument. I could never think less of you because of that."

"When David died, it killed me inside. However, I knew that you needed access to what was rightfully yours. Plus, taking care of you was putting my parents in the poor house. All the AAU basketball teams, camps, and travel was killing them. I made enough money to pay the bills and provide your basic needs, but the older you got, the more that started changing. Your shoes alone were enough to break me. David's dad tried to give me a hard time about it and had demanded the blood test. I understood that though. After the truth came out, he was pissed. He wanted to meet you, but after the way he cursed me for filth, I didn't feel comfortable with that."

"Noah said he would take me to meet him after his tour ends. I could have met him in Houston at the concert, but I didn't go, because Jess and her fiancé were there."

She lifted her head and frowned slightly. "Was that your decision?"

"Yeah. I can't control my eyes when I'm around her. I don't need that kind of trouble in my life. I'm doing my best to get over her. It hasn't been easy, but I'm making progress. She made her decision, and I need to be good with that."

"I'm sorry, baby."

"Naw, it's okay. I took a shot, and they don't always fall in the hoop. Sometimes, they're bricks. You still learn from them though. I should have moved quicker, letting her know how I felt about her. I played around for at least three months, trying to decide if she was truly the woman I wanted. In that time, another nigga came along. Being that he was in her hometown and she was already acquainted with him, that left Nate the odd man out. They were best friends in school. So I supposed he was the man meant for her."

"Maybe, maybe not."

"She's engaged and pregnant. So I'm going to assume he is. Jess is very headstrong. Does she care for me? Absolutely. But she loves him. I have to move on. That shit ain't healthy."

"You're right. The woman that's meant for you is out there somewhere, baby. Just don't give up on love."

"What about you?"

"What about me?"

"Mama, I haven't seen you dating anyone... ever."

"I went on dates when you stayed with your grandparents for the weekend. Nothing just ever came out of it. Unfortunately, I truly believe David was my one, and I messed everything up. When you were two, I thought about reaching out to him, but he'd married Raquel. Even after they divorced, I still knew how much he loved her. I'd hurt him beyond repair. Telling him he had a son that was nearly five years old by then would only hurt him more. Don't be like me. I've given up on love since David died. Something inside of me died when he did. I never got to tell him how I truly felt about him, because I didn't realize how I felt until I no longer had him."

I pulled her close to me again and realized just how much we had in common with Noah and Raquel. It was crazy, and maybe that was what had attracted David to my mom. She reminded him of his Quel. Noah and I were definitely kindred spirits. He was more spiritual than I was, but we shared a lot of the same qualities. "Thank you for telling me the truth about what happened. We need to make a promise to each other, Ma."

She sat up and stared into my eyes, waiting for what I would say. "We need to promise to start living life to the fullest. You're a beautiful woman, so I know niggas checking for you. I'm going to start dating and going out again. When God made Jess, he didn't stop making beautiful women, nor was she the first. My one is out there somewhere, and I ain't gon' find her by pining after Jess. We gotta do this for ourselves. Your one is out there too. David wasn't your only option."

She gave me a tight smile then nodded. "You're right. Deal," she said, extending her hand to me.

I chuckled then shook it. "You better not renege."

"You either, re-nigger."

I fell out laughing as I thought about our favorite movie, *Welcome Home Roscoe Jenkins*. I nodded repeatedly. "I won't. Now, let's go enjoy this party and celebrate our new beginning."

CHAPTER 2

KENYA

"Taryn, you need help with anything?"

My sister turned to me as she pulled cookies from the oven. She refused to take advantage of all the money they were rolling in. She could have hired someone to do that shit for her, but she insisted on doing things herself for Brooklyn. They'd named her after Noah's first last name of Brooks since Noah's oldest daughter was named after his first name. I thought it was cute. She'd given her the middle name of Ariel, like her middle name.

"No. This is the last of them. Where's Arik?"

I shrugged. "Where is he always at? Work. He's supposed to be coming later today though. He had some last-minute shit he said he needed to wrap up."

She stared into my eyes. "Kenya, it's apparent that you aren't happy about that. Why are you putting up with it? You told me you talked to him about it already."

"Besides that, he's a good man. I don't want to hurt him."

"Maybe he *is* a good man, but not good for you, sis. Things not working out between the two of you doesn't mean either of you are bad people. It just means you aren't meant for each other. Look how long it took me to find the man that was for me. You're younger than me, not even forty yet. Quit wasting time though."

I rolled my eyes because she'd told me that shit before. Arik was a beautiful soul. He was kind, but his career was in place long before me. He was a doctor, and we'd been together for a little over a year... only a month or so before Brooklyn was born. When he wasn't at work, he was at a seminar or workshop out of town. The man was dedicated to his job. We met at a hospital. I'd gone to visit a friend and literally ran into him in the hallway.

My knowledge of medical terminology from my days as a nurse impressed him when I picked up the papers I'd knocked out of his hand. I hated that job, so I finally quit three years ago to chase my dreams. I was a singer, just like my sister, but I didn't necessarily crave the spotlight. I did background vocals. I'd worked on several albums last year, and this year was panning out to be a great one as well. I was working on TAZ's and Noah's next projects and had done work for three or four other artists as well.

"Man, something smells good! Lemme steal a cookie, T."

I turned to see Noah and Nate entering the kitchen. There was a woman in tow. She smiled brightly, and Nate introduced her as his mother, Sheila. "It's so nice to meet you," Taryn exclaimed.

As they got acquainted, I could feel Nate's eyes on me. When I turned to acknowledge him, he turned away. I supposed he thought I didn't have a peripheral. I could see his eyes traveling every part of me, and the attention heated my body tremendously. Nate was a very handsome man, but my body's response had caught me off guard. Every time I noticed him doing that, the feeling got more intense.

"Ms. Sheila, this is my sister, Kenya. My mom and Noah's mom will be here in a little while."

I smiled at her and extended my hand. "Nice to meet you," I said as I shook her hand and smiled.

"Nice to meet you also. You have a beautiful smile. You both do."

"Thank you," Taryn and I said in unison. "And you're a beautiful woman," I added as Noah walked away to tend to a screaming Brooklyn.

Nate slid his arm around her and said, "Gorgeous. I was just telling her that earlier. So now she knows I didn't just say that because she's my mama."

I smiled bigger. I could tell they were close. "Absolutely not. He didn't lie to you, Ms. Sheila."

I lifted my eyes to Nate's, and he held my gaze for a moment, then bit his lip. I quickly turned away and grabbed a cookie from the tray. I handed it to him. "Shh. Don't tell Noah," I whispered, then winked.

He licked his lips then gave me a head nod. I knew that tongue was excited, but it sure in the hell wasn't excited about that cookie. His subtle flirting didn't go unnoticed, and once he and his mom went back to the front room, I realized it hadn't gone unnoticed by Taryn either. "Kenya, girl! What the hell?"

I frowned and feigned innocence. "What?"

"Don't 'what' me! Nate was flirting with you!" she said in a harsh whisper.

"I noticed."

My cheeks heated. I couldn't stop them from doing so.

"And you're blushing about it! You didn't tell me you were feeling him."

I closed my eyes momentarily. "I think he's handsome. I haven't really been around him enough to be feeling him. Plus, I have a boyfriend."

"Bullshit. You've been around him enough. You have a boyfriend, with whom you aren't satisfied with. Well, now things aren't as one-sided as I thought."

I frowned harder. "What are you talking about?"

"He asked about you a lil while ago. Noah told him you had a man."

"Newsflash! I still do."

I rolled my eyes as she chuckled. "Why don't you ask Arik if you can go to some of the conferences or seminars?"

"Already did. He said no. He said we still wouldn't be able to spend time together, so it would be pointless. I would be bored when I could have just stayed home where I have plenty to do. I agreed. Mama could always use the company anyway."

"Don't be using me as an excuse, heifer!"

I turned around to see my mama and Mrs. Raquel making their way inside the kitchen. She immediately took a seat at the table as Mrs. Raquel laughed. Mama was at dialysis earlier, and Raqui, as Noah called her most times, volunteered to go pick her up. Although we weren't in Chicago, she had gotten to know the people at the center here, since we made frequent trips. They allowed her to get treatment here as well. That was extremely convenient, because it didn't limit the time we could visit.

I rolled my eyes. "Whatever."

"Why are you using me as an excuse anyway?"

"I wasn't using you as an excuse. That's what happens when you walk in on the tail end of the conversation. I was saying that when Arik was out of town, I could spend time with you."

My mama twisted her lips to the side, giving me a knowing look. Most of the time when we were together, I was complaining about Arik not wanting me to be with him. Taryn had a family to think about now. I didn't want to bog her down with my problems. It didn't make sense to be in a relationship and still be lonely. Arik had said he would be able to make time for a relationship. That worked out well for the first six months.

I often wondered if he felt like I wasn't his one. Maybe he was feeling the same disconnect I was feeling. As Mama and Taryn laughed and joked about it, I gave them a sarcastic laugh and left out the back door. I took a deep breath as I sat in the rocking chair and closed my eyes, trying to forget about Arik for now. My phone wouldn't allow that to happen though. It had chimed, alerting me of a text message.

Hey, baby. I'm sorry, but I'm not going to make my flight. There was an emergency at the hospital...

I refused to read the rest of it. I responded with one word. *Okay.*

There were no tears. I was used to being disappointed by him. I closed my eyes again just as I heard the back door open. I didn't feel like talking, but I knew Taryn would make me. She never had to twist my arm. All she had to do was hold me and hum. Although our dad left before I'd turned a year old and had died by the time I was four or five, I knew what his voice sounded like. Her voice sounded just like his.

It soothed me in ways I couldn't comprehend. Maybe it was because I was missing something I never had... kind of like Nate. I continued to rock and realized no one had said anything. I opened my eyes to see no one was standing there. That was strange. Maybe they were looking to see where I'd gone then went back inside. I didn't hear the door close again though.

I turned toward the door, and no one was there. Just as I was about to close my eyes again, Nate walked around through the gate with a purse. He smiled slightly. "You meditating?"

I chuckled. "Something like that."

"Your mom had forgotten her purse in Raqui's car."

I nodded as he continued to the door. Suddenly, he stopped and turned back to me. "You okay?"

"Yeah. Thanks."

He nodded and walked away again. When the door closed, I released a hard breath. Why was I holding my breath? The man was fine as hell, and my body was taking notice without me. My mind was far away from here. It was in Chicago, wondering why Arik thought he always had to be the doctor on call. My heart was there too, wondering if there was another woman he was seeing. At this point, it didn't even matter. I no longer wanted him as my all. Honestly, he was never my all. A side chick got more attention than I did.

I stood from my seat and decided to stop focusing on him and why he wasn't here. I was here to have a good time with my family, celebrating Brooklyn's birthday. When I got back inside, Noah's kids and his ex-wife had arrived. They were passing Brook back and forth. "Aunt Kenya!" Noelle yelled.

I chuckled as she ran to me. She was a replica of her father. "Hey, superstar!"

She giggled as she wrapped her arms around me. She'd released her album about six months ago, and it had gone platinum. She was so excited. Noah had her all over the country, doing interviews and making appearances. She was seventeen now, but she'd graduated high school early. That was why Noah had delayed her album a little bit. He wanted to be sure she would have the time without the hoopla of it all interfering with school.

When she pulled away, she asked, "You okay?"

I smiled. "Yeah, why do you ask?"

She side-eyed me. "Your smile isn't reaching your eyes. Plus, I can feel it."

Noah and his spiritually enhanced kids. "I'm okay, boo."

I kissed her cheek and gave her hand a reassuring squeeze. She kissed me back and made her way back to Brooklyn. I spoke to everyone who'd arrived and noticed Nate's mom and Raqui talking in the front room. Tears were streaming down both their faces. As I stared at them, Nate appeared next to me. "She needed this more than I ever knew."

I glanced at him to see him staring at them. I wasn't sure what he meant, but I didn't ask questions. I felt like he was talking more to himself than he was to me. "How long are you here for?" I asked.

He brought his attention to me, and his gaze was heating me up again. "I leave in the morning. I have a game in Philly tomorrow evening."

"Oh, that's right. I try to keep up with the schedule."

His eyebrows lifted slightly as I looked away. I was the outcast of my city because Chicago was not my favorite team. Dallas was. That was long before he had even joined the roster. "I know you ain't a Dallas fan."

"I am. I have been for as long as I can remember. Don't tell Michael Jordan."

"Girl, I ain't got access to that nigga!"

I walked away and laughed loudly, nearly bursting from holding it in. I didn't want to disturb Raqui and Sheila with my outburst. He chuckled too. "That's what's up. I'm glad I chose Dallas then so I can be a part of your favorite things."

"No you didn't reference Oprah when I just disrespected Chicago," I said, trying to keep the moment light.

He chuckled. "You catch on quick. I like that. Well, I know your favorite rapper ain't from Chicago either. At least your favorite singer is."

I smiled and nodded. As I attempted to walk away from him, he gently grabbed my hand. When I turned to him, he quickly released it. "My bad. I'm sorry. I didn't mean to be disrespectful."

I nodded and quickly got away from him. I was feeling him too, but I hadn't closed the door on my relationship with Arik. There was no way I would entertain him before doing so. Taking a deep breath, I found Taryn staring right at me. *Great.* Noah was welcoming more guests inside, so I went to the kitchen to be sure all the food was ready. When Taryn joined me, I said, "I don't want to hear it. That's why I got away from his ass."

She chuckled. "I wasn't going to say a word, but a brother has definitely made his interest known."

I rolled my eyes. "That man is six or seven years younger than me."

"And? Did you know Sonya is fifteen years older than Noah, nearly the same age as his mother? That didn't seem to stop her."

"I'm not Sonya, and Nate isn't Noah. Besides, they had a working relationship for at least ten years before they went there."

"Again, and? Why do you care about age? He's in his thirties. Grown as hell."

I brought my hands to my face and took a deep breath. "I'm in my feelings right now. Arik isn't coming."

I felt her arms wrap around my waist, and she kissed my cheek. When she began humming, the soft cries left me. I knew what needed to be done. Arik needed to be in my past. Clearly, I wasn't a priority in his life, and I refused to keep making him a priority in mine.

CHAPTER 3

NATE

"Nigga, I know you turning up with me tonight. It ain't often you carry yo' ass to Baldamore," RJ said loudly.

"Man, I'on know. My flight leave out at six. That mean I need to have my ass to the airport no later than four thirty."

"If you would take advantage of me and Noah's private jet, you wouldn't have that shit to worry about."

Noah frowned as I chuckled. "When did you get a jet, RJ?"

"Nigga, the same day you did! All my fucking pain and suffering, I part own that shit," RJ said, causing me to laugh.

I swore it was the same shit every time I came here. It was obvious they were brothers. They gave each other a hard time at every turn. RJ hadn't gotten totally comfortable with me to give me a hard time just yet, although he said any brother of Noah's was a brother of his.

"Ryan, watch your mouth. Nate's mother is here. You wouldn't want her to think you're as ignorant as you sound," their dad, Rev. Charles said.

I chuckled as my mama said, "It's okay, Ryan. I love the carrying on these two do... language and all."

"See, Senior, everybody wit' it except you. I had forgotten you were here, Ms. Sheila. I apologize."

Mama nodded with a dismissive wave of her hand as RJ continued. He glanced at his dad, then said, "As I was saying, you owe me, nigga."

Noah rolled his eyes. "I don't have a problem with you using the jet, Nate. Real shit. RJ don't even ask. I look at the manifest and see the nigga name on the shit."

We all laughed as TAZ joined us with a clean Brooklyn. She'd torn that damn cake up and expressed just how rich it was in her diaper. We'd all laughed as TAZ had fake gagged when she sniffed her. "Now that the princess is clean, we can open gifts!"

RJ huffed as he stood to follow her back to the main area. "Why we gotta do this? Brooklyn ain't gon' even be paying attention."

Noah pushed him in the head as my eyes traveled to the sexy ass woman gathering the gifts. She damn near had me in a fucking trance earlier when I stared into her sad eyes. I didn't know what had happened to change her mood. She was happy when she got here. Since her man wasn't here yet, I was more than sure it had something to do with him. Her sadness had affected me though. I wanted to pull her in my arms and just hold her. When I grabbed her hand and she turned to look at me, I snapped out of it.

I was already on the verge of disrespecting Jessica's relationship. I couldn't jump from the skillet to the fucking frying pan. Kenya had a man, no matter how disappointed she was in him. I continued watching her, though, because I couldn't help myself. Her shoulder-length dreads were sexy as fuck, not to mention her milk chocolate skin, covering her five-and-a-half feet frame. At least, she looked to be about five-six. She could have been shorter.

It was her smile that first captivated me though. It was always big and bright. She resembled TAZ, but her eyes were smaller, and her cheek bones were higher. She wasn't a BBW either, but she wasn't skinny by any means. She had thick thighs that caught my attention the last time I saw her, and she'd worn leggings.

When she looked at me, I averted my gaze. That was the second time today she'd caught me staring at her. She probably thought I was a creepy ass nigga now. Although we'd been around each other a few times, we'd never had a one-on-one conversation until today. So, technically, she didn't know me personally, and I didn't know her.

"She nice, bruh."

Damn. RJ had caught me looking. I didn't have to turn to him to see who it was. No-fucking-body had a voice like that nigga. "Yeah, she is."

"She practically naked now."

I frowned and stared up at him. "What'chu talkin' 'bout?"

"You done stared the fucking clothes off her ass, nigga. Shoot your shot and quit being a punk."

I supposed my thoughts about him not being comfortable with me were out the window. "She has a man."

RJ looked around as if he were looking for him. "Where that nigga at? I ain't met his ass yet. If I ain't met him, then his ass don't exist. It's time she acknowledge that shit too. Again, shoot your shot."

I took a deep breath as TAZ began helping Brook open her gifts. The way that little girl screamed in excitement made everyone around her happy. You couldn't help but smile at the sight. After she'd opened a couple more gifts, RJ mumbled, "Tallest nigga in here and got the audacity to be nervous. If you don't fucking man up and tell that woman she belong to you, I'm gon' tell her ass for you."

I sure in the hell didn't want his ass interfering in my shit. I didn't think he would actually do it, but I didn't wanna take any chances either. As soon as they were done cleaning up and shit, I would approach her. "Man, shut the fuck up. I got this."

"Oooh, baby brother feeling himself."

He wrapped his strong ass arm around my neck, putting me in a

29

headlock. I didn't even try to fight his ass. Noah had told me plenty of stories about this very thing. "Come on, old man. I don't wanna hurt yo' ass," I said as Noah laughed loudly.

He released me and nearly pushed me off the stool I was sitting on. "I got yo' old man. Mess around and be on the injured reserve fucking with a nigga like me."

I slowly shook my head as I watched my mama enjoy her time with Raqui and TAZ's mother, Ms. Eunice. I could see that she would probably want to be around them a lot more now. She didn't really have a lot of friends back home. She was always around my grandparents and her other family members. She had a brother and sister on her dad's side, but they weren't that close. She also had a younger brother, but his ass was locked up for selling dope.

I made my way back to the front room and sat on the couch with the men while the women cackled in the kitchen. Noah said, "I'm sorry, Nate. I didn't get to introduce you to our people. That's Carrington, our uncle. Nathaniel, Karma's dad, over there, and that's Chad. He's more of RJ's boy, but we're cool too. Since they got here after the festivities began, I didn't get a chance to tell you who everyone was. They all know you though."

I chuckled. "I'm surprised they didn't introduce themselves then."

"Our people don't roll like that. They ain't finna intrude on your space unless invited to. They know what we as celebrities go through on a day-to-day basis."

"I don't go through that shit every day. I ain't as big as you."

"That's because you don't go nowhere," he said, causing me to chuckle.

As the room started to clear out, the women joined us. Surprisingly, Kenya sat next to me. I thought I'd made her uncomfortable. I figured she would want to be as far away from me as possible. When I glanced at her, she turned to me. "It's okay. Why are you acting like I make you nervous?" she asked.

"I'm not nervous. I just don't want to offend you. You have a man, and I'm obviously flirting. That's not good."

"It's okay. You haven't been disrespectful. You're a nice-looking man, Nate. I'm sure you can find someone else to admire though."

I frowned slightly. "I wanna admire you though. I can tell you aren't as happy as you were when you got here."

She glanced at me then brought her gaze to her hands as she played with her nails. "Can we talk privately, Kenya?"

She looked over at me and nodded. I took a deep breath as I stood, then helped her from her seat. I was shocked she agreed. The minute she turned her back, RJ scrunched his face and gave me a goofy ass smile. I almost laughed out loud. That nigga was crazy for real.

We went out the back door to the patio area and sat on the outdoor couch. She sat first, and I quickly sat next to her and grabbed her hand. "You're a beautiful woman, and RJ told me to shoot my fucking shot. I know you have a man, but I would be a fool to not know that your sadness has something to do with him. Noah said he was supposed to be here today. RJ said since he wasn't here, that nigga didn't exist."

"Tell RJ's ass to stay out of my business," she said with a chuckle. "Nate, thank you."

"You're welcome. I wanna get to know you, but at the same time, I don't wanna get to know you. You have a man, and if I get to know you without you ending up being mine, I'll be torturing my-fucking-self."

"Which is why I have to say no to that right now. When or if things change, I'll let you know."

I nodded repeatedly as I lowered my head. There was no way I would set myself up for failure like that, and I was glad that she refused to set me up for failure also. What I realized, though, was that she was feeling me too. Otherwise, she would have just said no without an explanation or hope for the future.

"I can respect that."

She brought her fingertips to my chin and lifted my head. She stared into my eyes, and I went for it. I brought my lips to hers and softly kissed her, then stood from my seat. Her eyes closed for a moment, then she stood as well. That was the sweetest kiss I'd received since Jessica's. When she kissed me back, I was shocked. I expected her to pull away from me. If that wasn't a promise for the future, I didn't know what was.

She grabbed my hand. "You're sweet, Nate. Thanks for this moment of tenderness. I needed it."

"Anytime," I responded, wanting to kiss her soft lips again.

When we walked back inside, TAZ nearly fell, like she was trying to eavesdrop. She and Noelle were looking at everything but us. "Y'all ain't fooling nobody, skeezers!" Kenya said.

I chuckled, then slowly released her hand and headed back to the front room with the guys. As soon as I sat, RJ went in. "Well? What happened, nigga?"

"Nothing. She has a man. She'll let me know if that changes."

"Mm hmm. You got gloss on your lips, nigga."

I quickly wiped them as RJ laughed loudly. "Man, that's the oldest trick in the damn book," Noah said. "You didn't have shit on your lips. You kissed her?"

"Just a lil peck," I said as I shot RJ the finger. "She thanked me for my tenderness, and we came back in."

"So she kissed you back?" Noah asked.

"Yeah, slightly."

They both smiled as they glanced at each other. Rev. Charles was just as confused as I was. He asked, "What?"

"He gon' tap that ass eventually, Pop," RJ responded.

Rev. Charles rolled his eyes. "I should've known better. The older y'all get, the worse y'all get."

I slowly shook my head. "I ain't tapping shit unless she totally done with that nigga. I can't go through another Jessica situation."

"You can't compare that shit. Jessica was single as fuck when y'all were involved. I can admit, she did you dirty. That shit wasn't on you. But you do have to move on. I understand your point though. Jess was fresh off a breakup when y'all met. She was vulnerable," Noah said.

"Yeah. I didn't go all the way with Jess until months later. She was still vulnerable though. She was fucking with the nigga she with now and hadn't told me. She didn't have to tell me. I knew when I stared into her eyes that night. She was giving me a goodbye fuck. She slept with me because she knew what she was about to do. She should've kept her pussy to herself." I glanced at Rev. Charles. "I apologize."

He stood up and put up the Baptist finger as we all laughed. He sat back down and said, "Ryan Junior is my son, but I accept your apology."

I nodded. "It doesn't matter that she gave it to me though. I was already in love with her."

The room fell into a comfortable silence as Brooklyn found her way to her daddy while wiping her eyes. She'd had a full day of fun and people to have fun with. All the kids in attendance were older than her, but no one could tell her that. They'd all packed her around at some point. The gifts she received were top shelf though. Noah's ex, Sonya, had sent baby girl a fourteen-karat gold sippy cup. Like... who made shit like that?

A lot of Noah's other friends had sent gifts as well, despite their absence from the festivities. It was a busy time for Noah, so he could totally understand their busy schedules. The house was full though, so it was a good thing everyone didn't show up.

The women came to the front and joined us. Kenya sat across the way from me and seemed to be in a heated conversation as my mama sat next to me. My eyes stayed glued on Kenya though. I could feel her pain from here. When I was finally able to tear my gaze away from her, I turned to my mama to see her staring at me.

"She's a beautiful woman, son," she said softly. "She needs time though."

"Yeah, I know. I just can't ignore her."

"Your heart is big. Just protect it, okay?"

"I will," I said to her, knowing if Kenya gave me any more attention, my ass would be ready to be all the way in.

She ended the call and stood from her seat and left the room. When I saw her wipe her cheek, my heart went out to her. I glanced over at TAZ and saw her watching her as well. She stood and left the room after her. I grabbed my mama's hand, doing my best to resist the urge to go check on her.

CHAPTER 4

KENYA

"Why did he even call? He'd already said he wasn't coming. This was something we could have discussed when I got home."

"I know. I'm sorry you're going through this," Taryn said.

Arik thought it was a good idea to call and reveal that he'd been seeing someone else. He thought it would be easier to do by phone than having to stare into my eyes and see my hurt. I deserved better. The crazy part was that he didn't want to break things off with me. He was convinced that he could somehow be everything I desired if I would give him another shot. *The audacity of his ass!*

"So now instead of me enjoying my next couple of days here, I'll be sulking, wondering what I did that caused him to step out of our relationship... wondering why I wasn't enough."

"This isn't your fault, Kenya. Don't blame yourself. He's a jack-ass... a fucking jackass."

While I knew it wasn't my fault, I felt like every woman that had ever been cheated on went through a moment like this. I'd given Arik my all, even when I wasn't getting his all in return. I tried to be everything I thought he needed. When he'd get back in town from his seminars and such, I would be waiting for him. I cooked his meals and gave him the thing most valuable to me… my time.

Taryn pulled me close and began humming. That shit wasn't helping right now though. The hurt was too deep. If anyone had a reason to cheat, it was me! He was the one that was never here to provide companionship or any of the things I needed from him. I hadn't had sex in almost a month. I was almost forty. There was no reason I should be in a relationship with a man I had to check after to make sure he was being faithful.

I was beyond that shit. Although I'd felt a disconnect between the two of us, knowing that he was getting something from someone else that I so willingly provided hurt like hell. If I would have been keeping the pussy from him, it still wouldn't have been a reason to cheat, but at least I would have understood it better. I was an open book with Arik. I gave him my time, love, affection, and my pussy. I was doing everything a wife did. Maybe that was the problem. I was giving him *too* much without proper documentation.

I pulled away from Taryn and wiped my face, thankful that I didn't wear makeup today. "Come on. I didn't come here to cry and mope around. I can go through those emotions when I get home."

When I got to the door to head back inside, I saw Nate getting something out of the fridge. I took a deep breath and went inside. Here was this gorgeous man, wanting my time, and I had a man in Chicago giving time that should have been mine to someone else. He peeked around the door of the fridge then went back to what he was doing. As I was about to walk through, he said, "Kenya."

Taryn's gaze softened like she would cry any minute, so I turned back to him to see he had poured me a glass of wine. A soft smile found its way to my lips as I approached him. He licked his lips and said, "I felt like you could use this. I don't know what's bothering you, but I heard wine could make anything better."

I brought my hand to his chest and just laid it there. Closing my eyes, I did my best to soak up his heart and his genuineness, then opened my eyes. "Thank you, Nate. It's a start."

He extended the glass to me, and I took it, taking a sip immediately. I nodded repeatedly. He grabbed my hand and led me to the bar area. I sat as he stood next to me, not saying a word. When I looked up at him, he gently caressed my cheek with his thumb then walked away. This man was passionate, caring, and gentle. Who ever knew a professional basketball player could be those things? All I could imagine was kissing his thick lips again, taking it a step further and grabbing the braids at the top of his head.

I glanced back to see him sitting back on the couch, but his eyes were on me. That man was showing me so much care. *Jesus.* I gulped my wine and headed upstairs. I couldn't take his intensity. I'd end up doing something I shouldn't, simply because I was hurting. Being alone right now was my best bet in order to get my spirit right.

WHEN I WALKED INTO MY LOFT, FLOWERS WERE EVERYWHERE. THAT only reminded me that I needed to change my locks. I rolled my eyes, knowing my allergies would be going haywire in a minute. Those damn flowers were covering every empty space available. Although I had basically moved to Taryn's place just to feel closer to her, I didn't give up my loft. My mail still came here.

I was independent and couldn't see myself fully living on her dime. I enjoyed perks of being her sister from time to time, especially after she and Noah got married over a year ago, but I refused to be a nothing ass individual. Although Arik knew I stayed there most times, I refused to give him a key to a house that wasn't mine. It was a stretch giving him a key to my loft. That showed how much I trusted him.

He stripped that away though. My phone had been going off back-to-back since I'd landed. If he had time to beg me up a wall, then he had time to devote to me before all this. I was done with this shit. I was going to be done anyway, but this erased the small amount of doubt still within me, thinking we could talk again. I thought I would give him one more opportunity to implement some changes to salvage our relationship before calling it quits.

I had a fine ass, rich tenderoni, trying to give me what I deserved: attention, affection, and love. I had my doubts about him as well though. I didn't want to be a rebound chick. His obsession with the woman in Noah's latest video wasn't a secret. I'd overheard Noah and Taryn talking about it on several occasions. However, he proved that he was paying attention to me. No one else seemed to notice my tears or heartache that night but my sister. If they did, they didn't say anything. He was showing me that I had his attention... all of it.

After pulling the mail I'd gotten from my lockbox from my purse, I went to the bar and sat to go through it. Despite what had happened, the rest of my time in Baltimore was enjoyable. Noah's family kept us entertained, especially RJ's crazy ass. Noah was funny at times, but whenever RJ was in the mix, he was even funnier. Laughs were endless. It helped me keep my mind off what was waiting for me at home. Watching the game Sunday evening had done that for me as well.

Nate was a beast on the court. However, experiencing his tender side only had me stewing in my juices as I watched him run up and down the court. I'd imagined him to be aggressive and a take charge type of person, only for him to be laid-back, somewhat quiet, and gentle. Noah and RJ watched me for almost the entire game. They didn't know I'd noticed them. I was more than sure their asses would be reporting back to Nate. Men were messier than women, quick to talk about what they thought they knew.

As I opened the contract from The Masked Singer, my phone rang.

When I saw Taryn's number, I answered. "Hey. I just sat at my bar. Sorry I forgot to text when I landed."

"That's okay. I just wanted to make sure you were safe."

As she continued talking about the party and how much she enjoyed my company this past weekend, my doorbell rang. I frowned as I said, "Hold on, Taryn. Someone's at my door."

"Really? Take the phone with you."

I chuckled, but she knew I didn't have pop-up visitors. I was almost sure it would be Arik, trying to catch up with me. He sprang that shit on me Saturday at my niece's birthday celebration, but now he wanted to be aggressive and talk. *Fuck him.* I checked the peephole only to see more flowers. I rolled my eyes and opened the door.

"Sir, I can't accept any more flowers. I already have to throw all these—"

When I saw the basketball stickers on the card, I said, "Never mind. I'll sign for them."

He gave me a soft smile and a stylus for me to sign his electronic pad. Once I signed and gave it back to him, he smiled then handed the bouquet to me. "Have a nice day, ma'am."

I nodded and closed the door, being sure to lock it. "What do you mean you can't accept any more flowers?"

I practically jumped out of my fucking skin. I forgot that fast Taryn was on the phone. "Shit, you scared me. When I got home, Arik had flowers all over the damn place."

Thinking about the fact that he had a key, I set the flowers down and went back to the door to put the chain on.

"And he sent more flowers?"

"I don't think these are from him. I think you know that. Someone had to give him my address."

She giggled as I pulled the card from the stem. I opened the envelope and pulled it out to read:

Hey, beautiful. I remember what you said about pursuing you, but I didn't like the way you looked when I left. I know the look of heart-break. I hope these cheer you up. Have a great day. Nate

P.S.- If things change, you know how to get in touch.

"Well? What did it say?"

I rolled my eyes. "Give me his number, nosy. Just that he hoped the flowers cheered me up and to have a great day."

She giggled excitedly and rattled off his number as I typed it in my phone. I knew his game schedule as well as he did. He had a game tonight in Dallas, then he would be in Miami this coming weekend. I was sure he would be glad for the three-day break. He would probably be at the concert Friday night, since Noah would be in Miami.

"Okay, Kenya. I have to go. Brook is whining, so she probably needs changing. Plus, I have to pack for Miami."

"Okay, sis. I'll see y'all out there Thursday. I can't wait to be on stage with you guys again."

"I love you. Now call Nate!"

I slowly shook my head. "I love you too."

I ended the call and stared at the number I'd punched in. Before losing the nerve, I hit the send button and listened to it ring. Just when I thought it would go to voicemail, he answered. "Hello?"

"Hi, Nate. It's Kenya."

"I know. Hey, beautiful."

My cheeks heated up. His voice was so damn tender. It would probably be a shock to my senses if I ever heard him yell. His voice reminded me so much of Michael Jordan's. Just a smooth baritone that I could imagine in my ear on a daily basis. "I wanted to thank you for the flowers. They're beautiful," I said as I glanced at the bouquet of all pink roses, tulips, and lilies.

"You're welcome."

"I suppose you're getting ready for the game tonight, huh?"

"Mentally, yes. I'm at home chilling for another hour or two. What are you doing?"

I glanced around my place and decided to be open with him. "I'm about to start packing shit up to take to the dumpster."

He was quiet for a moment. "The dumpster?"

"Yeah. My place was full of flowers when I got home. I almost didn't accept yours until I saw the basketballs all over the envelope."

"Well, I knew he would try to make up with you by sending flowers, so I told them to use an envelope to distinguish who'd sent them without being too cheesy. The lady was trying to add a plastic basketball to the arrangement."

I chuckled. "Yeah, that would have been a bit much. I'm not going to keep you. I just wanted to tell you thank you."

"You aren't keeping me, Kenya, but I know you probably just got home. TAZ told me your flight would be landing mid-morning Tuesday. Call me anytime. Is it okay if I save your number?"

I smiled slightly. "I expected you to. Otherwise, I would have called you anonymously."

"And you would have had to leave a message, because I wouldn't have answered that shit."

He chuckled, causing me to chuckle softly. "I'll text before calling. I don't want to interfere with whatever you have going at home."

"He cheated on me, Nate," I blurted. "That was why my mood changed that day."

I didn't know why I felt so comfortable telling him that. For some reason, I felt like I owed him an explanation, although I knew I didn't. "He told you that or did you find out?"

"He called me. Fucked up, huh?"

"Hell yeah. I'm sorry."

"Yeah, me too. I don't know why I spilled that shit on you, knowing you have a game tonight. Forgive me."

I closed my eyes as he said, "I'm glad you felt comfortable enough to tell me. Fuck a game. You can always talk to me about anything. Okay?"

A slight smile formed on my lips. "Are you really this perfect?"

"Shiiiid, apparently not since I'm still single."

Although he said it jokingly, I could hear the hurt in what he said. "Tell me about it."

"Have you decided what you're going to do?"

"About what?"

"Your relationship."

"What relationship?"

"Point taken," he said with a slight chuckle. "Okay. Well, wish me luck tonight."

"I will. I'll be watching."

"Good. That makes me wanna show out just for you, since I know you'll be keeping track of my stats."

"Mm. I can't wait to enjoy the show then. Have a great game, Nate."

"Thanks, Kenya."

He ended the call, and I held the phone to my chest like a lovesick teenager. After taking a deep breath, I looked around the loft and prepared to make several trips to the dumpster.

CHAPTER 5

NATE

As the team celebrated, I couldn't help but smile. LeClaren Foster had an amazing game. He was the star player of our team. It was guaranteed that whenever he had a good game, the win was ours, especially if a nigga like me stepped up as well. I didn't need anyone to remind me of my stats. I'd scored nearly thirty points tonight along with twelve assists and four blocks. A nigga was on one.

Several of my teammates congratulated me on a good game. I never really participated in the turnup after a game, at least not for the past year. I would much rather turn up with people I loved.

I grabbed a towel to make my way to the shower when I got stopped by a reporter. "Nate, you had an amazing game tonight!"

"Thank you."

"You usually have a decent game, but tonight was spectacular. What was your motivation?"

I smiled slightly as I thought about my words to Kenya. "God is always my motivator, along with my family. However, someone special assured me she would be watching. I told her that I would make sure I showed off for her tonight."

The reporter laughed excitedly. "And show off, you did! If she motivates you this way for every game, we can expect a run for the championship!"

"A run for the championship is always the goal."

"Thank you, Nate. Back to you, Jody."

I walked away with a smile on my face. Kenya Zenith was definitely my driving force. Talking to her earlier sparked my heart again. Sometimes I hated that I was so passionate. It didn't take much for a woman I was interested in to infiltrate my entire being. That was what had me getting hurt. Although I knew she said she was done with her relationship, I knew she was still speaking from a place of hurt and anger. She could very well choose to work things out with him.

After taking my shower and getting dressed, I was ready to get home and relax. When my phone rang, I looked at it and smiled. It was Jakari. I was pretty sure he'd seen the game tonight. "What's up?" I said as soon as I answered the phone.

"Nigga! You know what's up! You played a hell of a game tonight. You was firing at all cylinders and converting every shot you took! I'm glad your teammates kept feeding you when they saw that shit you was on!"

"Yeah, me too. Thanks, man."

"Don't be trying to sound all nonchalant and shit! I know you about to burst at the seams."

"I'm excited! You know that!"

"So where you going to celebrate?"

"My house. I'm tired as hell."

"Mm hmm. What shot you done took in your personal life? I heard that interview."

"TAZ's sister, Kenya."

"Ahhh, you said you was gon' holla eventually. That's what's up. Well, Jess went into labor yesterday. She had a little girl."

"Congratulations. Pass that to her for me."

"Yep. I will. See, I should've been at the game so we could have gone out tonight to celebrate."

I wasn't even focused on what he was saying now. I was thinking about Jess. She should have been mine, having my baby. Taking my thoughts back to Kenya, I smiled. I could imagine her being pregnant with a little Nate. Jakari had my ass jumping the gun though. I could easily move fast when I was for sure about my feelings for a woman, but I knew it was in my best interest to take my time this go 'round.

"You should've been, but I know your lady is pregnant. How's Yendi doing?"

"She's good. She's fourteen weeks along. I can't wait to see what she's having."

"I'm excited for you, man."

"A'ight. I'ma let you go. We gotta hook up whenever you come back to Houston."

"I'll be back in a couple of months. So I'll hit you up."

"That's what's up. Congratulations again!"

"Thanks, bruh."

Everyone else seemed to get more excited than I did. My emotions were running high for sure, but I expressed them in the moment. When the buzzer sounded, I expressed them on the court. Once my adrenaline slowed down, that was it. As I got to the caution light, my phone chimed. It was a message from my mama. *Congratulations, baby!*

I smiled slightly. My mind journeyed back to Jessica though. I still couldn't believe she'd had a baby. Letting go of her was hard, but after she finally told me to let go, I didn't have a choice but to honor her wishes. I supposed somewhere in the back of my mind, I was hoping she would see she made a mistake. Just by her giving me permission to be wherever she was had my hopes up. I would take her with the quickness... baby and all.

When I met her, she stole my breath away, and I was just starting to get that shit back. When I got to the caution light, I checked my phone again to see the text messages I'd missed. There were a few from my grandparents and a couple of relatives, but none from Kenya. I just knew she would have sent a congratulations or at least something acknowledging what I'd said in the interview, but there was nothing.

This loner life wasn't for me. I should have gone out with my teammates. Maybe it wasn't too late. I needed to go home first though.

Once I got home and had gone inside, my phone started ringing. When I saw Noah's name, I smiled. "What's up, bruh?"

"Shiiid, you tell me, superstar! Great game tonight!"

"Thanks, bruh."

"You're welcome. I linked up with some of my people in Florida, and we had a whole party while watching the game. Humble told me to tell you that he can't wait to meet you this weekend at the concert. He's gonna be there to perform 'Apple of God's Eye' with me."

"That's what's up. I can't wait to turn up with y'all." I was quiet for a moment, then I asked the dreaded question. "How's Kenya?"

"I don't know. I haven't talked to TAZ since before the game. She didn't say anything was wrong. Why?"

"Just checking on her. I mean, I know you know about her dude."

"Yeah, I know about that clown. How you call your woman while she's out of town to tell her you cheated on her? That's a nigga with audacity right there."

"Hell yeah. I... I mean, I just wanna know that her heart is okay."

"Call her then. I know you have her number. TAZ told me she called you earlier."

"She did, but I don't wanna bother her if she don't feel like talking."

"Nigga, if she don't feel like talking, then she won't answer. I think this is more about you. You feel something for her, but you scared to get caught up again."

I remained quiet, silently confirming his analysis of me. I didn't want to put too much effort into this if she wasn't going to put forth the same effort. I expected her to reach out since I'd had an amazing game, but I supposed I could reach out this time. "You right. I'll text her." After a brief pause, I said, "Jess had her baby."

"I know. Jakari told you?"

"Yeah. For once, I didn't ask how she was. He volunteered that information. I'm truly trying to move on."

"That's good. Well, you don't ever have to worry about me bringing her up in your presence or in conversation with you no time soon. Maybe you should tell Jakari to do the same."

"Yeah. I'll let him know next time we talk. Well, let me go find something to eat. A nigga is starving."

He chuckled. "A'ight. I'll see you Friday."

"A'ight."

I pulled some steak and cheese wraps from the freezer and threw them in the air fryer, then sent Kenya a text. *What's up? I hope all is cool on your end.*

I didn't want to be too personal, because I didn't know if she officially ended shit with her dude or not. I remembered what she said on the phone earlier… or rather what she insinuated, but that didn't mean she'd actually done it. There was still a conversation that needed to be had.

I started a playlist on my phone as I waited for her response. I mostly listened to R&B music. When "Calm & Patient" by Jhené Aiko came on, I closed my eyes, thanking God for His love. It was a song that always lifted me when I was feeling a way. I'd listened to it a lot since I'd withdrawn from the party scene. I listened to Houston rappers, occasionally, and Noah. I grew up on Slim Thug and Z-Ro. My mama used to love those niggas.

When my phone chimed, I grabbed it from the countertop to see a message from Kenya. I saw the sad faces, and I braced myself for what the message would say. *I'm so sorry, Nate. I missed the game. My ex showed up acting an entire fool because he saw me taking the last set of flowers to the dumpster. Then he refused to accept that I was breaking up with him. I thought I was going to have to call the cops. Had my mama not shown up, I would have.*

I took a deep breath. That sounded like a lot of drama that I didn't want to be involved in. I was more than sure he probably noticed the flowers I sent. Instead of responding to what she said, I sent, *Call me if you can.*

Give me a few minutes, and I will.

I blew out a heavy breath then got a plate to get my cheesesteak wraps from the air fryer as Noah's track, "How It Feel" came through. I bobbed my head and placed my food on my plate. That nigga knew he was talented as hell. I couldn't wait to turn up at the concert. I just hated that he would probably never perform two of my favorite songs from him again. "Dear Queen" and "Forever Mine" were the shit in my book. They were about his exes though.

His decision to take them out of his performance rotation was out of respect for TAZ, since one was written for his ex-wife, Jah, and the other was for his ex-girlfriend, Sonya. He'd loved both women with his life at one time. I didn't think TAZ would trip on that, though, since both songs were pretty big in his career.

I took a bite from the wraps I'd ordered from Sam's, and they were pretty good. Cooking wasn't my forte, so I tried to find shit that was easy for me to heat up. If it could be thrown in the air fryer, I was all for that shit.

When my phone started ringing, I rubbed my hand down my face, not knowing how this conversation would go. I grabbed it from the countertop as I swallowed what remained in my mouth. "Hello?"

"Hi, Nate. It's Kenya."

I slightly rolled my eyes. "You know you don't have to tell me it's you, right? Your number is saved in my phone, and I know your voice."

She chuckled nervously. I could hear the tremble in that shit. "Right. I'm so sorry I missed the game. I looked up the highlights, and you're trending. You showed out for me, and I didn't even get to watch. I'm going to watch tomorrow when I come back from the studio. I have to record some background vocals for TAZ."

"Are you still at home?"

"Umm... I'm at TAZ's place. Unfortunately, he knows where that is also, but he doesn't have a key."

"Are you going to file a restraining order?"

"I will if he comes around again and won't leave. He needs to respect my wishes. This evening was horrible. Honestly, I'd left him emotionally months ago. This shit just gave me the final push I needed to let him go so he can be great without me," she said sarcastically.

I nodded slightly. "Why is he in denial?"

"Because he's used to getting what he wants. He's an only child, rich, and an amazing surgeon. It doesn't help that people kiss his ass all the time."

"I'm going to assume you were one of those people at some point?"

She got quiet on me. Maybe I shouldn't have worded it that way. "Kenya, I didn't mean it like that. I meant that you used to hand him compliments all the time."

"For the record, I don't kiss ass. I'm a genuine person. If I give you a compliment, I truly feel that way about you."

"I apologize. I truly didn't mean it that way."

She took a deep breath. "I know. I feel like I know that much about you. So why aren't you out celebrating?"

"I only celebrate with people close to me."

"Hmm. That's interesting. What about your teammates?"

"We're cool. I only see them on the court though, whether that's at practice or at a game. I'm laid-back, but I don't consider many people close to me outside of my family. Noah is just a genuine person; plus, we have a common interest. It was easy to be open with him and now, RJ's crazy ass."

"You know we have that in common, right?"

"What? You're not close to many people either?" I asked.

"Well, that too, but I was speaking about our fathers. My dad died when I was about four, but he'd left my mom when I was a baby. I have no memory of him. He umm... was schizophrenic and killed himself. My mama raised me and Taryn alone."

"Damn. I didn't realize that. You think that's why I feel a connection to you?" I asked, trying to feel her out.

I didn't want her to think that I was attracted to her because of our similar pain. That couldn't be further from the truth, especially since I didn't even know that information. "No. I don't know why our chemistry is strong, but I don't feel like that's the reason."

"So, can I officially assume that your situation has changed, and we're getting to know one another?"

"Yes."

When she said she had left him emotionally months ago, that seemed to put my soul at ease. However, I knew that just because she was done, it didn't mean he was done. I would still have to be cautious. Plus, I had to admit that Jessica wasn't fully out of my system. If she texted me right now and said she was leaving Brix and wanted to be with me, I would be all in. I swore her pussy was laced with Fentanyl.

Her personality was magnetic. We were almost total opposites. She was outgoing, loud, and spontaneous at times. I was an introvert by nature, somewhat quiet, and extremely strategic. I knew what I wanted, when I wanted it, and how I would go about getting it. Planning my life had come natural to me. I supposed it was the Libra in me.

A slow smile graced my lips as I played through my schedule in my mind. "So, what are some of the things you like to do, Kenya?"

"Well… I love singing and anything to do with music, basketball, and skating."

"What type of skating?"

"Quite a few, especially rollerblading and ice skating. I also love spending time with family and my significant other. I believe… well, I know that's why I left Arik emotionally. We haven't been spending much time together. What about you?"

"Obviously basketball, spending time with family, watching movies, and I occasionally skate."

"No way. What type for you?"

I chuckled. "Rollerblading."

I glanced down at my food and decided to put it back in the air fryer until I was ready to eat it. That shit was probably cold as hell. Food no longer had my attention. A beautiful woman that I definitely wouldn't mind devouring had stolen all my attention, and I wasn't the least bit upset about that.

"I suppose, maybe one day, when the basketball season is over, we'll have to plan an outing."

I smiled. "A date, Kenya. We'll have to plan a date to go rollerblading. Sounds fun."

She giggled. "Right. A date."

I was coming on stronger than I anticipated, but I wasn't the least bit upset about that either.

CHAPTER 6

KENYA

"So, that's what you think of all the money I spent on flowers? You're throwing them away?"

"Arik, leave me alone. What you did, flowers can't make up for that. This was overkill."

"Just tell me you aren't totally done with me. I can make up for what I did. I'm so sorry, Kenya. The guilt of it all was weighing heavily on me, baby. I didn't have to tell you, but knowing I was deceiving you that way was eating me alive. Just please tell me you'll give us another chance."

"No! You cheated on me and had the bright idea to tell me by phone, while I was out of town! You stopped spending as much time with me because you said you always had to 'work' and go to out-of-town seminars. You had to work alright. You were working on another relationship!"

I dropped the flowers in the dumpster and took off back to my loft, only to see him running behind me. When I got to the door, I hurriedly tried to open it to slip inside, but he pinned me against it. "Why are you running from me?"

"Because I don't want you in my space! You apparently were sick of being in my space anyway! That's probably why I hardly ever see you! You should have been in Baltimore with me! Where were you, Arik? Huh?"

"Please, just open the door and maybe we can talk things through. I can answer all the questions you have for me."

Closing my eyes briefly, the lone tear trickled down my cheek. That only pissed me off more. I didn't want him to see my pain. I didn't want him to know how his betrayal had hurt me and had me thinking I wasn't enough. My self-esteem had taken a hit. While I knew I wouldn't be in this space always, I didn't want him to confront me while I was in it, feeling vulnerable.

Despite all of that, I opened the door and allowed him in my space, to simply avoid my neighbors being in my business. When I closed the door, he wrapped his arms around my waist from behind, trying to kiss my neck, as I had a brief moment of weakness. My cries rocked my body. However, he failed to see that my breakdown was more about me than him.

I pulled away from him. "I'm so much better than this. I don't deserve the bullshit you just put me through! What is it that you think I don't do for you? Why did you cheat?"

"Kenya, that doesn't matter. What matters is that I fucked up, and I realize my poor judgment call. I need you in my life."

"You are full of shit! You've probably been full of shit since the very beginning of our relationship!"

He frowned hard as his eyes made their way to the lone bouquet of flowers on the countertop. "Who are those from?"

"None of your business."

At that moment, I was glad I had taken the card and put it in my nightstand. Nate didn't deserve to be dragged in the middle of this. "How dare you get pissed about my admission when you're clearly seeing someone else!"

53

"Fuck you! The only person in this room that has cheated is you! How dare you! I loved you with everything in me, Arik! For the past six months, almost, you've been distant, saying you had to work or go out of town. You knew time with you was important to me! You don't get to try to accuse me of anything but being too trusting of your ass!"

"I'm sorry. You're right. I apologize, Kenya."

"How long has this been going on?"

"That's not important."

"That long, huh? Get the fuck out of my place!"

"Kenya, please don't do this. I need you, baby. I love you."

I was obviously serving some purpose in his life, but I knew he didn't love me. He was trying to save face. We'd been photographed multiple times at different benefits and fundraisers. He'd painted me to be the perfect partner, supporting him in every aspect. I wasn't perfect, but none of what he said was false. I supported all his agendas and efforts, except this one. He had an agenda that I couldn't afford to be a part of this time.

"Kenya! Open the door! Baby, I'm sorry. Please don't shut me out."

I rolled my eyes as I continued packing like he wasn't banging on the door, disturbing all the neighbors. It was like he wasn't here long enough the night before last, trying to plead his case. After I told him to leave, he ended up staying another hour before my mama knocked on the door. We'd argued nearly the entire time, neither of us receiving an understanding of each other. My only understanding of him was that he was a selfish bastard that wanted his way, no matter who it hurt.

I had come back to my loft to pack for my flight to Miami. I was going to the concert, and hopefully, I would be able to attend Nate's game the next night. I didn't tell him I would be there, and he didn't ask. Our conversation from the other night had remained easy and laid-back, and we ended up talking for nearly two hours.

He was starting to fall asleep, but I still had to insist that he got some rest. I had enjoyed getting to know him. Knowing how close he was to his family was an extreme plus for me. I wanted to bring up Jessica, but I decided to save that for another time. My past issue was still causing ruckus, doing his best to disturb my fucking peace, like he wasn't the one who threw what we had away.

I kept packing like I didn't hear a thing, placed a call to request a squad car to my residence, then texted Nate. *Good morning. I hope your day has started well.*

My flight would be leaving in a few hours so I could get to practice tomorrow morning. I was only going to be on stage for two songs, the two songs Noah and TAZ did together. After getting my carry-on bag together and putting my toiletries in my luggage, my phone started ringing. It was Nate.

"Good morning, Nate."

"Good morning, beautiful. How did you sleep?"

Before I could respond, Arik started banging on the door again. I rolled my eyes as Nate asked, "What was that?"

"He's been banging on my door for the past fifteen minutes. I came here to get clothes," I said, not wanting to reveal I was packing for Miami.

"Have you called the police?"

"Yes. Right before I texted you. They should be here soon. I'm sick of dealing with him. We haven't really had a calm conversation for closure, but I can't stand to look at him long enough to do that."

"Why don't you do it by phone like he did?"

"That's an idea. We yelled at one another nearly the entire time he was here two nights ago. I just want to be done with him. I told him I was done with him, but he insists that I'm too vulnerable to make permanent decisions," I said while rolling my eyes.

There was another knock, and I heard, "Ma'am, it's Chicago PD."

"Why don't you call me back after you handle your business? I'll pack for my flight while I wait to hear back from you."

"Okay, Nate. Talk to you soon."

I ended the call as I made my way to the door. When I looked through the peephole, I saw Arik standing there with two police officers. The minute I opened the door, he said, "I can't believe you called the police."

"I told you, Tuesday, that I would if you came back. I want to be done with you and your cheating ass, Dr. Matthews."

I said his professional name so the officers would know who he was. The officers looked at him, and one of them stayed with him at the door as the other followed me to the bar area. "Hello, ma'am. Are you Kenya Zenith?"

"Yes, sir. I called to get him escorted away from here and to file a restraining order."

"Okay. I take it that there was a recent breakup."

"Yes. I broke up with him Tuesday, and he wouldn't leave. This is my residence. He was here for two hours. He would have been here longer had my mama not shown up. I had been telling him to leave since he'd first gotten here, and he refused. I told him if he showed up here again, I would call the police. He's been here for twenty minutes or a little longer."

"Is this your residence only, or did the two of you share it at some point?"

"This is my place. Let me get the lease information."

I walked away as I noticed the other officer speaking to Arik. Both officers were documenting. It didn't matter what Arik said. I didn't want him on my property or anywhere near me, period. After retrieving the lease agreement from my file cabinet, I made my way back to the officer that was taking my report and handed it to him.

Once he read over it, he asked permission to snap a picture of it. I didn't care what he took a picture of, as long as it would serve as proof to keep Arik away from me. He then began filling out more paperwork for the restraining order and had me sign the portions I needed to sign.

After all that was done, he stared at me, like he was trying to figure out who I was.

"Can I ask you a question?"

"Sure."

"Are you related to the singer, TAZ?"

"Yes, sir. That's my sister."

"I thought you looked familiar. You sing background for her sometimes, right?"

"Yeah. I take it you've been to a concert."

"Or two or three. I'm a huge fan. Don't worry, Ms. Zenith. We'll get this taken care of for you."

"I really appreciate that, Officeeerrr..." I said as I looked at his badge. "Atwater? I know you lying."

He chuckled. "Yeah. Very coincidental."

Now all I could think about was the TV show *Chicago PD*. Atwater was the whole reason I even watched the show. The officer standing in front of me was easy on the eyes as well. He licked his lips and smiled, and I couldn't help but smile back. Was he flirting with me? He handed me his card and said, "We will file this when we get to the computer in the car. If you have any questions or issues, feel free to call."

"Thank you, Officer Atwater," I said and giggled.

He slowly shook his head as a smile appeared on his face. Glancing over at his partner, I could see he was wrapping up as well and was about to escort Arik off the premises. "Kenya, I really am sorry about everything. I just wanted to right my wrongs."

"It's too late for that, Dr. Matthews. I hate it had to get to this point."

He nodded and walked out ahead of the officers. I rolled my eyes and mumbled, "Jackass."

Atwater turned to look at me before leaving. "See you at the next concert."

"Sounds like a plan. Thank you."

I supposed I wasn't as 'in the shadows' as I thought I was since he recognized me. Then again, I didn't have a very common last name, so he probably assumed I was related anyway. Taryn and I resembled, but I looked more like my dad than she did. When they left, I went back to my luggage, making sure I had everything together, then texted Nate. *Restraining order filed. Are you busy?*

I had about an hour before I had to leave for the airport. Seeing Nate and being free with him was all I could think about. After rolling my luggage to the door, my phone started ringing. A slow smile made its way to my lips. *Here's to a new beginning... hopefully, the journey to my one.*

CHAPTER 7

NATE

"Nate!"

People were screaming, and cameras were flashing as I made my way through the airport. This shit was getting worse. It didn't used to be so bad. Ever since my game had elevated and people saw my connection to Noah, it had gotten worse. That private jet wasn't sounding so bad now. The security team was in place, though, and I was thankful. I should have flown in with the team and avoided all this, but I wanted to get here earlier to chill out with Noah.

He said he and TAZ would be in Palm Beach tonight, so that was where I was headed. It was only a little over an hour from Miami. The team would be here later tonight. We would have a one-hour practice in the morning. After getting in the car that was waiting for me, I sent Kenya a message, letting her know I'd landed and was heading to my hotel to change.

I was a little nervous about the concert because Noah was planning something, but I wasn't sure what. The unknown tended to make me a little antsy. While I was sure it probably wasn't anything bad, I just didn't want it to be anything that would make me emotional, especially not in front of all those people.

Kenya texted back, telling me to be careful and have a good time with Noah. I wished I would have asked her to come along. After more thought about the situation, my mind kept telling me to slow down. She had a lot of drama going with her ex. Although she didn't say, I was pretty sure he saw the flowers from me. I had no intentions of being in the middle of that bullshit. With the way the media was following me these days, he would know about our attraction to each other before we could count to ten.

When I heard him banging on her door, everything in me wanted to hop a flight and get to her. My heart was already feeling a way toward her, and I didn't like that shit. I fell in love within two point five seconds, if I was already feeling somebody and I had the slightest inclination that they were feeling me too. I paced for an entire hour after getting off the phone with her, waiting to hear back and hoping she was okay.

Surely, she would think I was crazy and that I was on some rebound shit. My attraction to Jessica wasn't a secret to anyone close to me, or Jess for that matter. Kenya had probably heard Noah or TAZ talking about it. I noticed how beautiful Kenya was right away, but I didn't have any plans of pursuing anything with her at the time. She could have very well heard *me* talking about Jess to Noah.

I'd never dated an older woman, but I knew I could handle it. People in my family often told me I had an old soul. I was mature for my age because I mostly hung around people older than me. As a kid, it was rare I stayed overnight at anybody's house, because my mama didn't play that mess. She said she refused to possibly subject me to anybody's toxicity, whether it was intentional or not. If she didn't know somebody's parents, I couldn't even go to their house to play, let alone spend the night.

So my upbringing had unknowingly prepared me for Kenya and

everything she had to offer. I just hoped my upbringing could also ensure I used wisdom when dealing with her situation with her ex. I hated being gun shy when it came to my feelings. When it concerned a woman, I didn't usually hesitate about what I wanted. However, that shit with Jessica had me rethinking my second and third thoughts. Even with all that hesitation and second guessing, I still wished I would have invited Kenya out.

Once I was changed and looking fresh, with my gold and diamond chains hanging around my neck, I made my way to my car. I was happy Noah had set up my security, because I would have come out here naked, no security in sight, and got mauled. People in the hotel were taking pictures and waving. I gave a few head nods and posed for a couple of pictures then got inside the car.

Following my thoughts from earlier, I sent Kenya a text. *I wish I would have asked you to come out early with me. You're probably busy anyway. You'll be at the concert tomorrow though, right?*

I knew she sang background for them sometimes, but I didn't know if she would be making the trip. She was at the show I missed in Houston, so I was glad I didn't go. She would have had to see my attraction to Jessica play out right before her eyes. Her text came through as my car turned into the gated community.

You should have asked me. I'm not busy.

I was gonna have to stop tripping. I could have been holding her in my arms. This was a private residence, so I was more than sure no one would be sneaking pictures to exploit. I dropped my head back against the seat, mouthing, *fuck my life.*

When the driver opened the door for me, I surveyed the three-story Mediterranean style home. I was pretty sure these types of homes were even more popular in Florida. Palm trees lined the driveway. Everything about it looked inviting. Walking up to the front door, I could hear the noise inside, not to mention the music playing. I rang the doorbell, and surprisingly, Noah was the one to greet me.

"Bruh! You made it!"

"Yeah. What's up? This crib fly."

"It is, isn't it? I bought this house before I married my first wife. She still lives here with my oldest two kids."

"Oh! That's what's up."

"Everybody is in the backyard. Come on."

I followed him through the house, looking around in awe. This shit was nice as hell. When Noah slid the door open, I ducked my head to walk through it and saw a backyard full of people. I could feel myself somewhat retreating into my shell as he said, "Yo, everybody! This my lil brother, Nate Guillory! Y'all make sure y'all welcome him to Florida!"

People yelled and threw up hands in a welcoming manner as I chuckled. TAZ and Raqui immediately walked over to greet me, along with my lil niece. "Nay!" she said, shocking me.

I smiled big. "What's up, baby girl? When you learned my name?"

"She knew it last weekend. She was just being a diva since it was her birthday," TAZ said, enlightening me.

I chuckled and kissed her cheek then set her on the ground to play with the other kids. A woman walked up to TAZ and looped her arm around hers. I thought TAZ would introduce her, but she took the liberty of introducing herself. Upon further inspection, I knew exactly who she was. "Hello, Nate. I'm the one and only, Sonya Taylor."

She smiled big as Noah walked over, slowly shaking his head. He had a couple of men with him. "Nice to meet the one and only. The video vixen that set the tone for these lil girls out here," I said, gassing her up.

"I know that's fucking right. Noah been schooling you, huh?"

"Naw. I can't forget greatness. I used to watch those videos back-to-back on the weekends, wishing I could meet you. Look at me now."

She giggled and went up on her toes with her lips puckered. I leaned over and accepted the kiss on the cheek. "You're a cutie too.

Too bad both my daughters are already spoken for. This is my husband, Shawn."

He was one of the men that walked over with Noah. I shook his hand, then Noah introduced me to Humble. He was too excited to meet me and assured me he would be at the game Saturday night. As I was about to walk away to greet more people, RJ said, "I know like hell you ain't about to walk off without saying shit to the king of the hood, my nigga."

I chuckled and slapped his outstretched hand. I swore he was the same every time I saw him. "What's up, bruh?"

"Shit. Noah was taking forever with the food, so I had to go handle up on the grill."

I chuckled and was about to walk away again until the most beautiful woman emerged from the pool, rendering me speechless. She wore a bikini, displaying those thick ass legs of hers. The water was pouring from her shoulder-length dreads as she shook them. I swore she was moving in slow motion. I couldn't move another muscle as I watched her make her way to me with a huge smile on her face.

"Hey, Nate! Surprise!"

She laughed loudly as I scanned her from head to toe... slowly. I licked my lips and grabbed her hand. "Damn. You let me beat myself up, wishing I would have asked you to join me, and your fine ass was already here."

She blushed as RJ smirked and left us alone. I pulled her wet body to me and leaned over to hug her. "Nate, I'm wet!"

I chuckled, but my mind had gone a totally different direction. My fingers wanted to go exploring to find out. I kissed her forehead as she pulled away from me. She smiled big then pulled me with her to a chair. Several people greeted me on the way, and I politely nodded back, but a nigga had tunnel vision like a mug.

Once she sat on a lounger, I knew she expected me to sit next to her, but I straddled the chair and eased behind her. Her entire body looked to redden. "Please tell me I ain't making you uncomfortable," I said close to her ear, watching the goosebumps appear on her shoulder.

"No. I'm very comfortable, surprisingly," she said as she leaned back onto me.

I wrapped my arms around her then kissed her cheek. *Slow down, Nate! Slow yo' fast ass down!* I rested my head against the lounger before I started kissing all over her. My dick was starting to get stiff, and I didn't wanna push her away by jumping the gun. "You look beautiful, Kenya."

"Thank you. You look nice yourself. These shorts really show off your long legs. I've never seen you in shorts up close and personal."

"Thank you, baby. Damn! I can't believe you're here. I mean, I'm glad as hell though."

She turned to me and stared into my eyes. "So, tell me," she said, placing her hand to my cheek, sliding her fingers through my beard, "why didn't you ask me?"

I licked my lips as I stared back at her, not allowing my gaze to waver. "I didn't want to move too fast. You have shit you tryna wrap up. I have a habit of taking off for the races when shit feel right to me."

"I suppose you and Noah have that in common. I remember telling my sister to just go with what she felt when Noah had her on the fast track. I had to tell myself the same thing the other day. I want to be free to do whatever feels right to me, Nate. I know I have some shit going on, but I can promise you, my feelings are all for you."

My lips parted as she talked. Was she saying what I thought she was saying? I lowered my face to hers and softly kissed her lips. When I was about to pull away from her, she gripped my beard, forcing me to hold my position. "Are *you* free to feel though?"

I knew exactly what she was asking me. I wanted to say yes without a second thought, but my spirit wouldn't allow me to. So I simply said, "I'm trying to be. I'm sure you are aware of my hangup with Jessica Monroe. She's moved on… nearly a year ago. She has who she wants and just had a baby. It's time I move on as well. I want to move on with you."

She gave me a soft smile then puckered her lips again. I lowered my lips to hers and kissed her softly. This felt right, and I'd be damned if I would let an unhealthy obsession ruin it.

As I sat in VIP, waiting for the concert to get started, a barmaid brought me a bottle of water. I didn't drink alcohol the night before a game. Had the game been before the concert, I would have turned up. I couldn't risk getting carried away and feeling like shit tomorrow. Before I could get comfortable, though, a stage manager approached me and asked me to follow her.

I was somewhat confused at first, then I remembered Noah was doing something for this show. The nerves coursed through me as I followed the woman down the long hallway to the stage. VIP wasn't very far from the stage. When we got backstage, I immediately saw RJ. He smirked at me. "Noah good for surprising muthafuckas, so brace yourself."

I remembered how he surprised the Hendersons at the private showing for the video he did with Jess. There wasn't a dry eye in the place. I hoped this wouldn't be one of those moments. The music cranked up. One of his biggest hits that he opened every show with, "Hustlin'", blared through the speakers. When Sonya graced the stage, the crowd went wild.

I was a kid when that song came out, but I still remembered the video clearly. Every little boy my age had a crush on Sonya. Another woman with blue eyes joined her on stage, and again, the crowd went bananas. I recognized her as Exodus's wife. Exodus was a rapper signed to Noah's label. When Noah finally emerged, the noise was deafening. Fireworks were blasting off side-stage as the crowd rapped every word with him.

I waited to see if he would slap Sonya's ass like he used to back in the day, and surprisingly, he did. TAZ was cheering the shit on. They were relationship goals, for real. She was *that* secure in what they had that lil shit didn't matter. The fact that Sonya still had it was what was remarkable to me. That woman had to be sixty or older. I smiled slightly as the song came to an end, and Sonya hugged Noah and kissed his cheek.

The way my brother was loved in this industry proved how good God had to be. There had only been one person I knew of that bad mouthed him publicly. Everyone saw where that got him: on the outside, looking in. I was beyond proud to be connected to greatness. My father was at least able to witness greatness before he died.

Noah calmed the crowd down. "How y'all doing, Miami?"

There were screams all over the arena as Noah lifted his hand. "I got something special for y'all tonight. This is a song I've never performed or even recorded. It's a tribute to someone special in my life. I looked at him as a father, but his biological son is here with us. Y'all give it up for my lil brother, Nate Guillory!"

My eyebrows lifted as Noah gestured for me to come to the stage. When I walked out, I noticed the pictures of David Guillory flashing on the screen. My heart was overwhelmed. There was video footage of him playing basketball, him clowning around with Noah when he was a teenager, and him cheering Noah on when he graduated and performed. Those were all moments I'd wished I had with him. Even if I would have been in his life, he didn't live long enough to see me graduate, but he would have at least been able to see me following in his footsteps.

The fans' applause was so loud it felt like the arena was vibrating. It took everything in me to hold the emotions I felt on the inside. I refused to reveal my vulnerability in front of all these people.

However, when I saw a slide of me playing basketball paired alongside David playing as well, I couldn't help but let the tears fall. We'd driven to the basket exactly the same way.

Noah put his arm around me as I watched in awe. RJ joined us on stage and stood on the other side of me as if they were propping me up for a moment. The way the film went back and forth between David and me... my father was amazing. Something so small meant so much to me. It was like he lived through me on that basketball court. I'd noticed similarities in the way we played, but to see them back-to-back and paired together like this made it seem as if we were the same person.

I looked a lot like David as a grown man. It wasn't as noticeable when I was a kid. Noah left my side to engage the crowd then announced, "Y'all give it up for Sheila Green, Nate's mother."

When my mama walked on stage and came to me, I could no longer hold my emotions. She'd helped Noah with this moment. That was how he got all the video footage of me from my days in AAU and little league basketball. I leaned over and hugged her tightly, then lifted her from her feet. I did that often when I was feeling emotional, so she knew to expect it. As I buried my face into her, I listened to Noah's lyrics.

Daddy, you meant the world to me
Taught me how to talk to girls and respect them as queens
While your relationships were turbulent to say the least
You didn't hesitate to impart your wisdom in me
You told me this industry could swallow me whole
That they were sharks, looking to milk me for everything I was worth
Not to give in to their demands if it didn't represent me
Not to bow down to nobody on this wretched earth
If you only knew you had another son
You would have been so proud to witness the man he's become

He is you all over again, but an even better version
All the good you possessed is in him, your biggest conversion

I smiled big and lowered my mama to her feet. I held her hand as I rocked with Noah and RJ. It was like RJ was his hype man for this song. I believed it was to keep his emotions in check, because RJ was an entire fool.

When the song was done, I looked at the screen to see a picture of me in my basketball uniform, holding a basketball at my side. There was a faded picture of David behind me, like he was about to hug me, and he'd added wings on him, insinuating he was my guardian angel.

I closed my eyes briefly and took a deep breath as I nodded, and the crowd applauded. I turned to Noah and hugged him tightly. This moment had freed me emotionally. It felt like I was sharing all those moments with my dad, and I was beyond happy that it was an issue that I was now at peace with.

CHAPTER 8

KENYA

A
s soon as the songs I was singing background for were done, I made my way to VIP to be with Nate. That song Noah had done for his father was beautiful and had brought me to tears. I didn't even know the man, but looking at the slides Noah had put together made me feel like I was a part of all the momentous moments that flashed on the screen. I knew Nate probably felt the exact same way.

Seeing him come apart on stage was so emotional. The fact that I could relate to what he was feeling only made me want to get to him even more. Relaxing in his arms nearly all evening yesterday was so romantic. Feeling him softly kiss my cheek or shoulders as we talked made me feel cherished as a woman. He was perfect for me. His mother needed to be thanked for playing a vital part in who he had become.

My heart was still on my sleeve. I'd been vulnerable because of my situation, but having Nate in my space felt so right. We talked about nearly everything, and nothing about that felt weird to me. I was comfortable baring my soul to him, giving him all of me without him even asking me to. Freedom in love was powerful, and I was experiencing all the love he had to offer in a short time.

His aura was powerful when he allowed you access to it, and I loved that everyone *didn't* have access to it. He reserved it for the woman he felt passion for. I was blessed to be that woman at this moment, and it couldn't have come at a better time. With what had happened, having his assurance and tenderness kept me sane. It kept me from doubting myself and what I had to offer. He told me he wanted to overdose on my goodness, and that shit produced a shiver all over my body.

When I got to VIP, I saw Nate standing close to the railing, vibing with Noah. I quickly made my way to him and wrapped my arms around him from behind. He didn't face me right away. He grabbed my hands and lowered his head to kiss them. I could feel him take a deep breath as I rested my head on his back. This felt like a dream I never wanted to wake up from.

He turned around slowly as Noah ended the song he was performing and leaned over and kissed my lips. "Those runs you hit in the background were fire, baby. You have a gift. I need you to sing to me later. Your voice comforts my soul."

"Gladly. Whatever I can do to bring you peace, I'll do."

He gave me a soft smile then turned back around, pulling me in front of him as Noah began his next song. I thought my sister was blessed when God led Noah her way, and had prayed for the same thing, thinking Arik was the one. However, Nate was proving that I had it all wrong. He swayed behind me, and I could feel his dick hardening. I'd felt it yesterday when I was resting against him at the poolside. The man was blessed beyond measure, but I didn't expect anything less, being that he was six ten.

His hands rested on my hips as I subtly rolled them against him. I closed my eyes as I felt him lean over to my ear. "Listen, baby. I'm trying not to move too fast with you, but you making this shit hard. I wanna show you intimacy without breaching your gate to heaven, but damn if I don't wanna lick those streets of gold."

A chill surged through my body as I turned to him and slid my hands up his chest. "As long as it doesn't feel forced, I'm with it. Every moment with you has felt natural. I refuse to let my doubts about timing, bad relationships, and self-worth get in the way of my happiness. As long as you're an addition to my happiness, timing isn't important. I feel your sincerity and genuineness, so let's not hold anything back."

I closed my eyes as he lowered his face to mine and gave me the tenderest kiss I'd ever received from anyone. When I felt my body lift, I pulled away slightly. He'd picked me up, and his arms were wrapped around my thighs, right beneath my ass. I slid my arms around his neck and kissed him again as he swayed to Noah's music. "You Need a Different Breed" was one of my favorites by him.

Most of these dudes just tryna pull ya panties to the side
I want that and mo'
I'm talking get in your mind
Make love to your dreams
And fondle your thoughts

And just like that, I was gushy between my legs. Nate's hands had drifted to my ass as I kissed him with a passion I hadn't released in months. *God, what am I doing? Do I really wanna take us to this level?*

Nate pulled away from me and closed his eyes for a moment. Lowering me to my feet, he grabbed my hand and led me to a seat while the entire arena was still turned up. When he sat, he pulled me down on his lap. His mama was nursing a drink and grooving in her seat. She gave me a wink as I smiled at her.

I brought my attention back to Nate to find him staring at me. His gaze was so intense I literally wanted to straddle him right here in front of his mother. *My God.* I was so glad Arik fucked up. This man was going to be my undoing.

71

He slid his hand to my ass and said in my ear, "I'm not willing to go where I *think* you're taking us without a verbal confirmation that this is what you want. I'm sick of casual ass sex. If my dick enters your life, so does the rest of me. I need to know if you ready for something serious. I am. I been fiending for the shit, honestly. You just got out of a relationship, no matter how pathetic and fucked up it was. Make sure you take all the time you need for *you*. Allow your heart time to recuperate, because mine can't sustain another break so soon."

I stared into his eyes, doing my best to ease his doubts. "I'm ready, Nate. Like I told you before, I left Arik emotionally months ago. Before he called that day, he'd texted, saying he wasn't going to make it to Baltimore. I'd told TAZ about how unhappy I was about us never spending time together. He was always 'working' or at some conference or seminar. There was rarely ever much time for me. I'm ready for something real. Everything about you feels real. It's no accident that we are both here in this moment."

I gently rubbed his cheek with my hand as I heard RJ say something in the mic, causing the crowd to laugh. Nate and I couldn't be further away from what was going on. We were so wrapped up in one another, someone would have to come pull me off him for me to notice them. The only thing that made me hesitant or somewhat nervous about him was that he seemed too good to be true.

No one was perfect, but Nate hadn't exhibited one single flaw. This conversation we were having, even amidst all the noise, proved just how perfect he was. He wanted to make sure I understood his position to where there would be no confusion later. I'd never had a man make the extra effort to clarify things between us. If I gave a green light, they ran through it with gusto, whereas Nate wanted to proceed with caution.

He nodded his head repeatedly, then said, "Well, let's enjoy ourselves for now. We came to see a show, and Noah and RJ are down there putting on one. We can table this for another time. Just know that

I'm feeling the fuck out of you, and I'm gon' make sure you feeling every inch of me too."

My body shuddered as he stood with me in his arms. When he set me on my feet, I noticed Taryn standing next to me. She'd finally made her way to VIP. I knew she would be making her way backstage before the show was over to sign autographs though. I smiled at her, but her weak attempt at reciprocating didn't slide past me. I looped my arm through hers and asked, "You okay?"

She shook her head as Noah stared up at us. I wasn't sure what happened at that moment, but he stopped the show and walked off stage. "Taryn! What's wrong?"

"Mr. Brooks passed away. Noah's grandfather died."

"Oh no. I'm so sorry. How did he know?"

"We have a spiritual connection like none other. He can sense when I'm feeling a way. Apparently, he sensed just how serious this was. Raqui had told me to wait until the concert was over to tell him. Grandpa is already gone. Noah's dad messaged us, so Raqui took Brooklyn on the flight with her to keep her company."

I hugged my sister as RJ tried to calm the crowd, along with Noah's manager, Russell. When Noah appeared at the entrance to VIP, Taryn left my arms to run to his. Nate came to my side and asked, "What happened?"

"His grandfather passed," I said softly.

When I saw Noah crumble, falling to his knees, it hit me right in the heart. His grandfather played a huge role in raising him. He was almost like his father instead of his grandfather when he was growing up. This had to be hard for him. Taryn went to the floor with him and consoled him the best way she knew how. She hummed as he clung to her. I couldn't help but cling to Nate the longer I watched them.

I looked out at the crowd to see the confused faces and disgruntled fans who didn't know that Noah's world had just stopped. After a few moments and a few boos, Russell appeared back on stage to let the fans know that Noah had a family emergency. He also asked them to keep Noah and his family in their prayers.

RJ walked through the entrance, helping Noah and Taryn to their feet. "Come on, y'all. We gotta get to the airport."

I stared at Nate as he grabbed my hand to escort his mother and me out of the area. The minute we got to the hallway, I turned to him and said, "I'm gonna stay for your game. I'll fly out Sunday morning. That was when I was supposed to head back to Chicago. I'm gonna see if there's a flight to Baltimore instead."

"Are you sure? I'm sure they could all use you right now."

"I'm sure. Noah's family will all be there. I'm sure Taryn, his ex-wife Jah, and Sonya will all be there to cook and offer the family comfort since they were all here to see his breakdown. Right now, I need to be with you. I need to make sure you're good with where we're headed before I leave."

He nodded and leaned over to kiss my lips then followed behind Noah and Taryn. We would probably ride in the same limo since we were all staying at the same hotel. Confirming my suspicions, RJ turned to us and said, "We can all ride together."

When I saw how red his eyes were, I knew just how hard Mr. Brooks's death was for the both of them. Noah's grandfather was like a grandfather to RJ as well. Seeing their depressive state pulled at my heartstrings. The way Noah's head hung and his locs framed his face would be a vision I wouldn't forget anytime soon.

The camera's flashing at this moment ignited my fury though. I wanted to really go off on these media personnel, knowing that these pictures would surface on the web for the world to see. Noah's moments of grief and hurt would be scrutinized by people who didn't have a clue what was going on. That was the part of the business that I absolutely hated.

Once we were in the car, we rode to the hotel in silence as I held Nate's hand and Noah allowed Taryn to comfort him.

———

Noah and Taryn immediately packed bags and left last night since Noah had flown privately. I stayed in my room and talked to Nate by phone until we were both ready to crash. Here it was, six a.m., and I was wide awake, staring at the ceiling. I wanted to stay with Nate so badly, but since he didn't offer, I didn't ask.

I didn't want to seem like I was being pushy. He was trying to take things slow because he was afraid I would hurt him. I had the same fears about him, but I couldn't let that rule me. He was so in love with Jessica Monroe, and he'd just recently stopped pining over her, according to Noah. We were in the same boat, both hurt by love but wanting to move on to find it again.

As I contemplated calling him, my phone rang. I grabbed it to see he was calling me. I smiled as I answered. "Good morning."

"Good morning, beautiful. Umm… can I come to your room? I need to see you," he said softly.

"Mmmm… really? Of course, you can. I'm in room seven fifteen."

"Okay. I'm on my way."

"Okay."

I ended the call and quickly hopped up to brush my teeth. I wanted to take a shower, but I knew I wouldn't have time before he arrived. Instead of abandoning it altogether, I started running it, then went to grab my robe off the bed. I quickly put it on and tied it then took off my bonnet. As I threw it to the nightstand, there was a knock on the door. *Shit!*

I pulled my locs from the twist tie they were in and fluffed them out as I made my way to the door. I put the tie around my wrist and peeked through the peephole to see Nate standing there. I quickly opened the door, stepping aside to let him inside. He smiled as he passed me. Once the door closed and I put the lever across it, I turned to find him standing there in his basketball shorts and T-shirt, staring at me.

He licked his lips and said, "Hey, beautiful."

I knew I was blushing. My face was hot as hell. "Hey, handsome," I said as I made my way to his embrace.

He lowered his stance and softly kissed my lips, then lifted me in his arms as I giggled. This way was probably more comfortable for him, being that he was so tall. This was the second time he'd lifted me like this, wrapping his arms around my thighs to where I couldn't circle my legs around him. I felt like he was doing that on purpose. He was trying to keep the pace consistent. If I wrapped my legs around him and I felt his dick on my middle, it would be full speed ahead.

He was wasting his time though. I was going to take it there regardless. He was so damn sexy and passionate. I couldn't help but kiss his lips. That was going to lead to the kiss deepening. We weren't in public, so we were free to let this go wherever it wanted to go.

"I can't wait to see you rooting for me."

"I can't wait to see you play live."

I kissed his lips again, and he allowed me to slide down his body, freeing me from his grasp. "So why are you up so early?" he asked.

"I was hoping to see you before you left for the arena."

"Mm. So why didn't you say so?"

"I know you're trying to take your time. I didn't want to seem pushy or clingy."

He gave me a slight smile as he sat on my bed. He pulled his bottom lip into his mouth and tilted his head, gesturing for me to join him. I didn't waste any time getting to him. When I did, he slowly untied my robe. It seemed as if my breathing went on pause as he opened it to find me in my bikini styled underwear and a silk camisole.

"Kenya, I need to know you want this as bad as I do. I don't give a fuck about that. I like a clingy ass woman because I can be a clingy ass nigga. Devoting my life to the right woman is all I want. I want to shower her with love, affection, and diamonds. You feel me?"

My body shivered at his words. "I feel you. Just so you know, I don't give a damn about material things. I just want a clingy ass man that adores me."

His hands slid over my stomach to my waist as he pulled me between his legs. "Mm. That's a fucking turn on for me. I just pray that you are as ready as you say you are, because I'm a whole ass vibe. I feel like you are too."

"I am, so I pray that you're ready as well. We both have a past filled with heartbreak, each with one of those being recent. The simple fact that we are drawn to one another at a time like this scares me. I'm praying that it isn't because we're vulnerable, but because this is genuine. There's only one way to find out though. I wanna give this all I've got, Nate. I didn't just develop an interest in you last weekend. I've always been interested."

As I spilled my heart to him, his gaze never left mine, but his hands had journeyed to my ass. He gently caressed it as I spoke, making my pussy gush. He had big hands and long fingers, so I was more than sure he could feel the heat and moisture he'd ignited.

"Damn, Kenya. Same here. My heart was somewhere else, but I noticed you from the first time we met. You aren't a rebound for me. I've always been interested too. My situation just wouldn't allow me to pursue you then. Come here, baby."

He licked his lips as he gripped my thigh, pulling it next to him. I straddled his lap, and his hands went back to my ass to hold me in place. Just as I thought, I felt his erection against me, and my body immediately slid against it. My eyes fluttered as my clit stiffened, hoping to feel everything he had to offer. I wanted him so badly I could barely focus on anything else when he was near. So this conversation was definitely going to be cut short.

I was struggling to keep my eyes open, so I allowed them to flutter closed as my hips subtly rolled against him. When I felt him nibble at my nipple through my top, I grabbed his loose braids atop his head, sliding my nails on his scalp. He stood from where he was sitting, and I immediately wrapped my legs around him.

He turned around and got in bed, hovering over me. When he lifted my camisole and licked my nipple then gently sucked it, a soft moan escaped me. Sliding my hands up his back, I pulled his shirt over his head, causing him to pull away from me momentarily. Seeing his tatted body took me places I had no desire to come back from. "Nate, you are so sexy."

He gave me a slight smile then pulled at my camisole. I sat up, allowing him to pull it over my head. "Damn, baby. So are you."

He brought his lips to mine and kissed me like he never wanted to let me go. When he pulled away and headed to my neck, I allowed my head to fall back and a sigh of passion to leave me. There was no way any woman could feel this sort of passion and let it go easily. *No fucking way.*

He continued south, licking and kissing my body hungrily until he got to my underwear. His eyes lifted to mine as his fingers slid into the waistband. I lifted my hips, and he slowly pulled my underwear over them. His gaze left mine and went to the treasure between my legs. When he licked his lips, I knew I was in trouble… trouble that I had no desire to get out of.

His eyes lifted and stayed on mine as he lowered his head between my legs. That nigga stared at me while he licked my pussy. I nearly detonated all over him before he could even get started good. When he released a deep moan on my clit, I lost it. I grabbed ahold of his hair, lifted my hips, and released a passionate scream as my orgasm flooded his face.

It had been so long since I'd been pleased orally, my pussy was probably in shock. Arik hadn't gone down on me in nearly seven months. Nate continued lapping up my juices like ain't shit happened.

His grip on my thighs got tighter as he sucked my clit, causing my body to convulse. I was holding on to his hair for dear life when my pussy squirted out her excitement.

He pulled away slightly and slowly shook his head. He stared at her for a moment, then gently pat my clit, causing even more to release from me. "Naaaaaate... fuck!"

"Mm hmm. Give me all of it, Kenya. All of this and all of you, baby. I promise I'ma take care of all of you."

My body trembled even more than it already was as the tears built up. I swallowed hard as he stood from the bed and pulled a condom from his pocket. "After last night, I knew I wouldn't be able to focus tonight without tasting you. My dick refused to be left out though."

He dropped his shorts then stretched out his boxer briefs and pulled them over his erection. I went up on my elbows and stared at his shit in awe. My eyes rolled to the back of my head at the sight of that thick ass four iron he pulled out of his shorts. "Oh shit, Nate. I'm a fan."

He chuckled then bit his bottom lip as he strapped up. "I'm a fan too, baby, a number one fan, and from now on, the only fan."

He came back to me, immediately assuming the position. When his dick slowly breached my gates, my body welcomed him. My pussy was already spasming. My hands journeyed to his back and slid to his ass, pulling him deeper. He swiftly grabbed my hands, bringing them over my head, then pushed into me, taking my fucking breath away. I wrapped my legs around him as I yelled, "Oooh fuuuck, Nate!"

"Let me handle this shit, Kenya. I'm your man now. We're consummating this shit. This pussy is mine, whenever I want it. You hear me?"

"Yeeeeesss, loud and clear. I'm down for you. I'll be ready whenever you are."

He pushed further into me, lifting my hips from the bed as he continued to pin my arms over my head. He lowered his head to my nipple, and I came without warning as his dick destroyed my insides in the most pleasing ass way. I screamed out my pleasure as he released my arms and brought one of his hands to my neck.

He didn't know it, but slight choking was my shit. I began rolling my hips harder, throwing the pussy at him with every stroke. "Oh fuck!" he yelled.

He quickly rolled to his back, pulling me on top of him. I immediately brought my hands to his chest and rolled my hips like I had something to prove. Nate smacked my ass cheeks at the same time, slightly lifting me from his dick. I started a slower bounce on him as a frown made its way to his face. He continued to stare at me though.

I couldn't take it. Closing my eyes, I continued to let his dick breach my soul while he fucked me back from below. The man had skills. The way he rolled his hips, driving the dick into me, showed just how experienced he was. The head of his dick dragged against my G-spot with every down stroke.

"Kenya, I need to see your soul, baby. Open your eyes."

He slowed his thrusts as I opened my eyes. God, it felt like he was making love to me. That was impossible when I knew he barely knew me. But again, he had gifts that seemed to make the impossible attainable. Pulling me to him, he wrapped his arms around me and slow fucked me like he loved me. My nipples slid up and down his chest. The friction was stirring my deepest desires and feelings for him, threatening to have them overflowing.

It felt like my body was turned inside out where he could see where every one of my spots were, because he was hitting them all. I was so overwhelmed with pleasure I had no choice but to release the tears in my ducts. *Damn. How the fuck he have me crying?* Before either of us could address it, my orgasm poured from me, soaking him.

As I screamed, he covered my mouth with his, forcing me to slow down and enjoy the overtaking. My hips wanted to wind out of control, but he forced me to maintain the same pace and enjoy euphoria a little longer. When he released my lips, he moaned as his eyes rolled. "Fuuuuck!"

The goosebumps appeared on his skin, and his veins were more pronounced as he reached his climax. Still, his pace didn't increase. He continued to slow fuck me right through that shit. He didn't have to worry about me not giving him my all. I was so fucking sprung off this one session he would have to pry me off his ass so he could get to the arena.

CHAPTER 9

NATE

"This shit is so fucking addictive Shit!"

Kenya and I were going at it in the shower. I had to be to the arena in exactly one hour, but I couldn't keep my dick out of her walls. I had her in the corner, digging all the goodness out of her. She was taking me like a champ, cumming every five minutes. Seeing the tears grace her cheeks let me know that we had some serious chemistry.

Every time I was free, she was going to find me in her space. This woman was amazing, and I couldn't believe God would bless me this way. I just hoped she was my one and not *the* one to take me for everything I had. Dismissing that thought, I continued to drive into her beautiful body.

I'd taken my time to wash every inch of her, learning her curves and noticing every beautiful blemish. She adorned a couple of stretch marks on each side of her hips, that spot that all men loved, right where her thighs met her hips. Watching how her titties bounced with every thrust was threatening to take me down for the second time.

I'd only brought one condom though. She was a fiend for my dick just like I was already one for that wet shit between her legs. Just that quickly, we threw caution to the wind like we'd known one another for years. She trusted that I was clean, and I trusted that she was too, especially since she used to be a nurse. She would know if something wasn't right with her body. *At least I hoped she would.*

"Kenya, fuck!"

She was holding on to my hair, and that shit brought out the beast in me. All ten inches of me had graced her insides at one point. I knew I couldn't do that in this position until I trained her shit to accept me. Either way, this was some of the best pussy I'd ever been in. If things went according to plan, this would be the last pussy I ever graced with my magnificence.

"Nate! I'm cumming! Oh my God!"

She released her goodness on me, and the temperature increased significantly. I pulled away some to look at the action, seeing that she was squirting all over me. I could feel my nut rising just from watching her pussy's reaction to me. "Your pussy loves me. You good for my ego."

She opened her eyes and pulled my face to hers, kissing me passionately. I swore she loved me. This shit was so intense. I quickly pulled her off my dick and grabbed it, squeezing the head. When she went to her knees and opened her mouth, my shit shot out of me while I was still squeezing the head. "Oh fuck!" I yelled as my seed shot all over her face.

I took mental snapshots of that shit as she backed up under the spray, still on her knees. I yanked her up from the floor and joined her under the spray. She wrapped her legs around me then kissed and licked my neck. "You need to get cleaned up so you can go, baby. I'll be here after the game to celebrate with you."

"You right. I don't wanna leave you though. Fuck! You got me, girl," I said as I bit her earlobe.

I lowered her to her feet and washed my beard and dick. She

decided to get out after she washed up so I could concentrate. Shit, she had me gone as fuck. I knew that would happen. I was desperate for love, and I hated feeling that way. Those months I didn't talk to my mama had only made that shit worse.

When I got out the shower, I checked the time to see I had thirty minutes to get to the arena. We were ten minutes away, so I would still get there on time, hopefully. My coach would be pissed that I didn't ride the team bus, but I needed Kenya. I was backed up, but that shit had gotten painful after the tease from last night.

Noah's loss had killed the moment. We didn't try to recreate it or force it after that. It allowed us to get more acquainted by phone, talking about our dreams and some of the things we wanted out of life. She'd mentioned her age several times during the conversation. I had to kill that shit and let her know her age didn't mean shit. It was my first time being with a woman that much older than me, but I told her it would be perfect since I had an older mindset and disposition.

Once I dried off, I walked out into the room to find Kenya completely dressed. She giggled as I scanned her from head to toe. "I didn't want to tempt you. I'm going to leave when you do so I can get something to eat. I'll probably get to the arena early. Is that cool?"

"Yeah. I'll let you know where to enter once I get there."

After slipping on my drawers, shorts, and T-shirt, I made my way to her and kissed her pretty lips. She pulled away and said, "Go. I don't want you to blame me for being late."

I chuckled. "I'm gon' blame you regardless."

She twisted her lips to the side as I leaned over to kiss her again. "I can't wait to see you after the game. Can I take you out? Are you cool with being seen with me?"

"Absolutely. Who do I need to hide from?"

That was just what I wanted to hear. This was about to be public. I was more than sure I would be hearing from Jakari not long after. That was my boy, but talking to him was still somewhat hard. Since I was actively pushing Jessica out of my system, talking to him always brought her back to my thoughts. It had been hard not to reach out to her to tell her congratulations on her new baby or to scroll her IG for new posts, but I did it.

"Hell yeah, baby. See you later, okay?"

"Okay."

She followed me to the door, and when I got to it, I turned back to her awaiting lips. I smiled at her beautiful face and kissed her puckered lips. "Have a great game, handsome."

"You here, so I'm sure to show out. See you."

I walked out of the door before I couldn't leave. When the door closed, I took a deep breath. I felt good inside, and I could only pray that this was it for me. I couldn't stay single with all the love I had to give. The way things had gone this weekend with Kenya, I knew it wouldn't be long before I was professing my love for her. I fell easily when it felt right. This was beyond right. It was perfect.

"FOUL ON NUMBER THIRTY-THREE!" THE REF YELLED AS I GOT UP FROM the floor.

I had been fouled hard when I drove to the basket. It somewhat dazed me because I'd hit my head on the floor. The entire crowd had 'oooh'ed' when it happened. My teammates were about to go apeshit on that nigga. The referees upgraded it to a flagrant foul once they reviewed it. I was down there for a minute, but once I got up, I'd looked toward where I knew Kenya was seated and winked. I wanted her to know I was okay, although I was still somewhat off balance. The plus was that the ball still went in, so the free throws would be an extra cushion in the point spread. Then we would get the ball back.

The problem was when I went to the line, it looked like two hoops were there. I shook my head as I closed my eyes and before I could get ready for my shot, my coach called a timeout. I made my way to the sideline, but not before stumbling. "We should have called a timeout immediately," I heard someone say.

Everyone had surrounded me, and the team physician was checking me out. "You may have a concussion. We need to get you checked, Nate."

I nodded slightly. The headache was coming on, I supposed since my adrenaline was slowing down. As I stood, two of my teammates propped me up on either side and escorted me to the locker room as the crowd stood to their feet and applauded me. I wasn't sure of my stats, but I was glad the game was almost over. We were in the fourth quarter with five minutes left. It was only a ten-point game though.

I turned to Hosea and said, "Y'all seal the deal, man. Don't let this shit slip through our fingers."

"We got it, Captain. You just focus on getting better. We gon' need you."

I nodded as the trainers helped me to the locker room. When we got to the end of the hallway, I saw Kenya standing there behind a security guard with tears streaming down her cheeks. She quickly wiped them and said, "Twenty-eight points, thirteen assists, three blocks, and ten steals."

Although she didn't say anything else, I knew she was worried. I could see it in her scrunched but lifted eyebrows, not to mention the tears. "Thank you, baby. I'm gonna be fine, okay?"

She nodded as I went inside the locker room. I wished she could have come in with me, but I would see her once the game was over. Hopefully, whatever was going on wouldn't have me sitting out too long, maybe only a game or two. I would be back just in time for post season play. We had a real chance at a championship this year. As Noah would say, Satan was a liar, and he wouldn't keep me from claiming what was mine.

By the time they'd run all the necessary tests, they'd ruled it a mild concussion. The doctor recommended a two-week break. That would put me missing eight games. I wouldn't be able to go back until the first game of the post season. He also said that if my symptoms eased up after a week, I could go to practice and see how I felt. If I was good, he would release me earlier.

That meant I couldn't celebrate the win with my baby tonight. We ended up beating Miami by eight points. There would be no screen time for two days. They said I should be okay to fly out tomorrow, though, since there was no bleeding, and the injury was minor. My vision was already better. I just had a nagging headache.

Once I was able to leave, I walked out of the locker room to see Kenya seated in a chair in the hallway. I gave her a slight smile as she stood and made her way to me. She grabbed my hand and pulled me to the chair she was seated in. She stood in it to be face to face with me. I chuckled slightly as she puckered her lips for a kiss.

She brought her hands to my face and softly kissed me as cameras began flashing. *Fuck!* She quickly hopped off the chair, and I shielded her from the vultures. We were surrounded by security, so they kept them from getting too close. The flashes had my head pounding though. By the time we got to the car, I rested my head against the seat.

Feeling Kenya's soft caress on my face had me opening my eyes. "I want to believe that you have a concussion. How bad is it?"

I figured she suspected it. That was why she didn't allow me to bend over to kiss her. "It's minor, baby, but I have to sit out for at least a week. The doctor suggested two but said I could go to practice after a week and play it by ear. No screen time for two days. I can still fly out tomorrow."

"Damn, baby. Can I stay with you tonight?"

"You didn't have to ask. I don't know why you didn't check out of the room you were staying in."

She giggled, then said, "I actually checked out earlier. They are holding my luggage behind the desk. I just wanted to see what you would say. Had you said no, I would have just gone to the airport tonight instead of tomorrow morning."

"Damn. You always welcomed to be anywhere I am. You feel me?"

"Yes."

"So, I have to go home first, but I want to join you in Baltimore. Are you going to stay until the funeral?"

"Yes. The funeral will most likely be next weekend. I'll check with Taryn tomorrow morning before I leave. They were supposed to be making plans today."

"Okay. That gives me a couple of days to recoup. I should be able to fly back out on Wednesday."

"I think I'm gonna stay with you. I want to fly back to Houston with you."

My eyebrows lifted. "For real?

"Yes. I told you I was clingy too. After this weekend, I don't want to be without you if I don't have to be. I don't have any studio sessions until next Monday. Let me come and take care of you."

"Shiiiid. My kind of woman. I appreciate you, baby, but I totally understand you going to be with TAZ and Noah. We're still new, and—"

She put her fingers to my lips. "We're new but so serious. I need to be here for you. I will make sure my mama gets to where they are, and I will see them when you do... Wednesday." She kissed my head. "Now stop talking for a little bit. We'll talk more when we get in bed, and I hold you in my arms."

"You gon' spoil me."

"Gladly, Nate. Gladly."

CHAPTER 10
KENYA

I held Nate literally all night. He was still laying on my chest with his arms wrapped around me. Even in this position, I'd slept soundly. I'd helped him shower, and that shit was hard as hell. I wanted to take advantage of him so bad. His dick was hard and ready for me. The nigga even had the audacity to ask for it, knowing that all activities were a no-go for a couple of days.

He squirmed some, then I felt his lashes flutter against my chest. The man had lashes that I would kill for. It never failed. Men mostly always had long lashes. They didn't need that shit. Such a waste. Now, here I was, wishing mine were longer. He slowly lifted his head and stared at me. "Good morning, sweetheart. How are you feeling?"

He gave me a soft smile. "I feel okay, baby. I just need some Ibuprofen for this headache."

"No, baby. You need Tylenol. Ibuprofen can cause your brain to bleed with a concussion."

"Tylenol usually doesn't work for me though."

"They didn't give you anything stronger?"

"Just Tylenol Three. That shit like eating candy."

"I'm sorry, Nate, but no Advil, Motrin, or Ibuprofen. That could put you out indefinitely. One thing I know you love as much as love itself is basketball. I can't have you risking what you love, baby."

"Okay. I have to see a doctor before we leave Houston too. They sent my scan to him this morning. His office is expecting it, although today is Sunday."

He stood from the bed, and I quickly stood behind him, putting my hands at his waist to be sure he had his balance. "How do you feel now?"

"I'm good, baby. Just hungry as hell."

"Okay. Well, let's handle our hygiene so we can get you packed and ready for our flight."

"What time is it?"

"Five. We have two hours. I'm gonna order breakfast after I brush my teeth. Any special requests?"

"I like omelets. I'm good with all vegetables and meat. I'll take French toast or pancakes, whichever it comes with."

"Got it."

I went to the phone and placed an order for room service as he used the bathroom then brushed his teeth. Thankfully, I was able to get a ticket for the flight he was on to Houston. I supposed, being that it was after spring break and before summer, the flights weren't full. I couldn't get a seat next to him, but I wouldn't be far. Maybe someone would switch seats with me. The team was flying to Toronto for a game there. They'd left late last night.

I was sure that not being with the team would start to bother Nate, so I was glad that I made the decision to be with him instead of going to Baltimore. After I placed our order, I sent a text message to my sister. Although it was still early, I knew she would see it whenever she woke up.

Hey, Taryn. I decided to stay with Nate after his injury last night. We will both be there Wednesday evening, I believe. Let me know when the services will be. Also, let me know if there is anything you need me to do before then. I can imagine your hands are full. I know Noah is probably taking this extremely hard.

Before I could set my phone down, I saw the bubbles appear, indicating she was responding. As she did, I could hear Nate's phone going off. I was more than sure his mother was worried. He didn't talk to anyone last night as far as I knew. He wasn't even supposed to look at his phone for two days. I'd have to be sure to make the calls he needed me to make and respond to the messages he needed me to respond to.

My phone chimed, indicating Taryn had responded. *Hey, sis. Thank God you're staying with him. How is he? Raqui had said they probably banned him from staring at screens for a couple of days. Noah is handling it better than I thought he would. He has his moments though.*

He's okay. Just a nagging headache. I'm sure I'll be making calls and text messages for him later. I love y'all. Our flight leaves in three hours, so I'll text you when we land in Houston. Love you.

After responding, I set my phone down, and Nate came out of the bathroom. I smiled at him and stood to go brush my teeth. He wrapped his arm around me and kissed my head. "Okay, go relax, baby. The food will be here in about fifteen more minutes. I'm going to brush my teeth so I can kiss your lips."

"A'ight."

He went to the bed, and I went to brush my teeth. When I heard him talking, I rolled my eyes. He had to have looked at that phone for him to be talking. I slowly shook my head as I heard him say, "I'm okay, Ma. I know."

She'd left after the concert because she had to work yesterday. She had taken time off for it and had planned to make a few of his future games. I didn't understand why she still worked with as much money as Nate made, but I supposed I sort of understood. His money wasn't necessarily her money. Taryn had said that Noah's mom was a pharmacist and had continued to work long after Noah blew up.

When I left the bathroom, I stood in the doorway and stared at him with a slight frown on my face. He sat up in bed. "I know. My mama was calling, and I needed to assure her that I was okay. It won't happen again."

I twisted my lips to the side as he chuckled. He extended his phone to me. "You hold on to it. The passcode is zero three one eight two zero zero seven. That was the day I found out David Guillory was my father."

My eyebrows lifted as I approached him and took the phone from him. "You're giving me your passcode?"

He pulled me to him, wrapped his arms around my waist, and rested his head on my chest. "I ain't got shit to hide. My phone dry as fuck."

I glanced at the screen, and my eyebrows lifted even more. "Umm, I don't call nearly a thousand unopened text messages dry, Nate."

"It's dry when those messages ain't from people I wanna hear from. You can delete all that shit. I ain't gon' ever read it."

"Well, you just suffered an injury. Some of these messages could be from people you care about that are checking on you."

"Yeah, you right. We'll go through them later, if you don't mind."

"I don't mind. I'm here to help you with whatever you may need."

"What if I need you how I had you yesterday morning?"

I pulled away from him. "Not today. Maybe tomorrow. You need rest and water the most right now."

Before he could respond, there was a knock at the door. "Room service!"

I smiled at him as I pulled away. He stood and followed me to the door. "Just in case you need help with the tray."

"I'll make two trips, Nate. You shouldn't be lifting anything either."

"Lawd, woman. You acting like I'm on the verge of being a paraplegic."

I giggled as I opened the door. He rested his hand at my waist and a camera flashed. "Shit!" he yelled.

I was sure the flash hurt his eyes. I frowned at the worker with the tray. "How could you let this happen? How did they even get access to this floor?"

He quickly gave me the tray and took off without answering my question. After making sure the door closed, I brought the tray to the table in the room and went to see about Nate. "Baby, you okay? I'm gonna call and file a complaint. The delivery guy, José, clearly allowed that person access to us."

"I'm okay. That flash just ignited my headache again though."

"Okay. Come to the table so you can eat."

I helped him up and held his hand as he made his way to the table. After setting his omelet and pancakes, picante sauce, and syrup in front of him, along with his orange juice, I grabbed my phone to place a call to the front desk. Before I could, I received a text message from Taryn. *Umm… you and Nate are trending.*

I frowned and immediately went to my web browser without responding to her. I typed in Nate Guillory, and the first thing that came up was a picture of me standing in a chair outside of his locker room, kissing his lips. I rolled my eyes and said, "I know you can't have screentime, but we're trending."

I could see his eyes widen in my peripheral as I scrolled the article. They knew who I was, which was strange in itself. I usually stayed under the radar. My name was listed and my affiliation to TAZ. I supposed since I'd been singing background for Noah and TAZ, all that shit went out the window. The article was speculating about a budding romance and had even brought up Jessica Monroe as being a past love interest of Nate's.

"Well, I mean, I knew it would happen when the picture was taken at the arena. Is that the one online?"

"Yeah."

"What's up? You feel a way about it?"

"No. I just don't like people in my business, especially people I don't know."

"Unfortunately, in the entertainment industry, you better get used to it. They'll go to crazy ass lengths to uncover a story if you have one worth telling. When they realized David Guillory was my father, it was all over the place. Thankfully, I was already in the NBA, playing for Dallas. I can honestly say that my hard work got me there and not who they knew my father to be."

I made my way to him and grabbed his phone from the table to slide into my pocket so he wouldn't be tempted to use it when it vibrated. The name on the lock screen gave me pause, and he clearly noticed it. "Why you turning red?"

"Jessica just texted you."

His eyebrows lifted, then he frowned. "What she want? Read it."

It was my turn to lift my eyebrows. This was a woman he was in love with and could possibly still be in love with, and he wanted me to read the text. That let me further know that he indeed had nothing to hide. I unlocked his phone and opened the message. Before beginning to read it, I glanced at him and asked, "Are you sure?"

"Yeah. Come here."

I sat on his lap, and he wrapped his arms around me. Bringing my attention back to his phone, I read aloud, "Hi, Nate. I know I said that we couldn't talk anymore, but I had to check on you. I saw the high-lights from the game last night, but I haven't seen anything regarding your condition. Is everything okay?"

He nodded but didn't say a word for a moment. "Okay. Thanks, baby."

"Do you want me to respond to her?"

"Naw. Check and see if there's a message from Jakari. If there is, you can respond to that one. He'll fill her in."

I nodded and scrolled the many messages and came across one

from Jakari that was sent last night, not long after he sustained the injury. "There's one," I said as I opened it. "Nate... shit! I know you won't see this message for a while, but when you can, please let me know you a'ight, man. That shit looked bad. We're praying for you."

He nodded again and said, "Respond with, thanks man. I'm okay. Just a slight concussion. I can't look at a screen for a couple of days, so my lady is sending the message. Tell Kenya hello. Thanks for your prayers."

I side-eyed him. He was making sure Jakari didn't say anything out of pocket or about Jessica. So I said, "I'm not putting all that."

He shrugged his shoulders. "Suit yourself. He's gonna keep talking."

He went back to his breakfast as I attempted to call the front desk again, only for a message from Jakari to come through. I thought the man would have still been asleep. It wasn't even six in the morning here yet. If he was in Texas like Jessica, it was even earlier there. Nate glanced at me and said, "Told you. What did he say?"

I rolled my eyes as Nate chuckled and opened the message. "Damn, nigga. How long you gon' be out?"

I responded, *Around two weeks. By the way, this isn't Nate. I'm only relaying the messages and his responses.*

Oh, shit! This must be Kenya. Nice to somewhat meet you, baby girl. Tell my boy congratulations.

"What all you and that nigga saying?" Nate asked, claiming my attention.

I smiled. "I told him that I wasn't you, just someone relaying the messages, and he automatically assumed it was me." Going back to the phone, I read, "Oh shit! This must be Kenya. Nice to somewhat meet you, baby girl. Tell my boy congratulations."

Nate chuckled. "Tell him I said thanks."

I responded, *Nice to somewhat meet you as well. He said thanks.*

"Who is Jakari anyway? How does he know Jessica?"

"He's her first cousin. I met them the same day, nearly a year and a half ago."

I nodded, then set his phone down and finally made a call to complain to the front desk. I could see Nate staring at me as he ate with a slight smile on his face. After I ended the call, he said, "Shiiiid, if you knew the sports entertainment industry, I'd hire you to be my agent."

I chuckled and finally sat down to eat my breakfast. We had to get a move on it if we were going to be on time for our flight. The way we'd dived into this relationship was unbelievable. It was like, yesterday morning, we were brand new, and today, it already seemed like we'd been together for years. I glanced at him as I stuffed my face to see he was finishing up his omelet. *Damn.* He was still perfect… a hint of stubbornness but perfect.

CHAPTER 11

NATE

When we got to my house, I took a deep breath and closed my eyes. My mama was already here, and I knew she would be trying to baby me in front of Kenya. I should've had Kenya call her for me so I could tell her that she would be joining me, but it didn't cross my mind until now. Kenya had me gone. The only thing on my mind was hugging up to her all day. She was so relaxed in this already.

When Jessica had texted, my heart rate had damn near climbed to the mountaintop. While I was trying to forget about her, I hadn't just yet. I did my best to hide my emotions when Kenya said so, but I believed I made the right decision by having her respond to Jakari instead. He would let her know that I had a lady now, so she wouldn't text again. I should probably block her number like I did her on IG, especially now that I was with Kenya. If there was an emergency of some sort, Jakari could be our middleman.

I was hoping that telling her to check Jessica's message would ease the tension I saw fill her, and it seemed to, especially when I told her to respond to Jakari instead. Offending Kenya or having her doubt me wasn't on my to-do list. My goal was to build her trust in the relationship we were embarking upon and to eventually have her fall in love with me.

"Baby?"

I opened my eyes and glanced over at Kenya. I gave her a smile and kissed her lips to try to assure her I was okay, then opened the door. I walked around the car to open her door as well, but she was already standing there, waiting for me to join her. "Kenya—"

"I know. I'm just trying to be cautious. Don't worry. I don't have a problem with you opening every door I come to. You can rest assure this won't happen often."

I smiled then kissed the top of her head as I saw my mother make her way to the porch. She had a stunned look on her face, and I could only hope that she would act like she had some sense. My mother didn't have the greatest relationship with women she'd met in my past, but that was a long time ago. She'd never met Jessica.

After the driver took our luggage from the trunk, I grabbed the handle and rolled the suitcase on the cement as Kenya grabbed the duffel bag. She slid her hand to mine, and I brought it to my lips and kissed it then held it until we got to my mother. "Hey, Ma."

"Hey, baby. I'm so glad you're okay," she said as she brought her hand to my cheek. She glanced over at Kenya, and said, "Hi. I didn't know you would be coming home with him."

Kenya immediately caught the shade. I could tell by the way her head fell to the side. "It was a last-minute decision. I was going to be going to Baltimore until his injury. I decided to change my flight late last night to be with him and make sure he was okay."

"You should be with your family during their time of bereavement. I could have taken care of Nate."

"Well, I'm trying to establish something with Nate. I wanted to show him that he's my number one priority. Besides, technically, it's my sister's in-laws. We're both going to go Wednesday. They won't need me any sooner than that."

My mama nodded, but I could see the ice in her veins. "Mama, chill out. You cooked?" I asked as I walked past her, pulling Kenya with me.

"I am. There's a chicken in the oven that I'm baking, broccoli and cheese casserole, and dinner rolls. I didn't cook a lot because I didn't know you would have company."

I glanced at her, trying to give her silent communication to kill that shit, but she was staring at Kenya. "I'm sure there's more than enough for all of us," I said, then kissed Kenya and led her to the stairs to go to my bedroom.

"Nate, I can lift the suitcase up the stairs. It's not that heavy."

"Kenya—"

"Nate. Do you want to be out longer than necessary? Let me help you."

I took a deep breath and allowed her to pull the suitcase up the stairs. Once we got to my bedroom and I had closed the door, Kenya turned to me. "Your mother isn't happy that I'm here. If my presence is causing trouble, I can get a flight to Baltimore. I won't be upset."

I frowned at her. "What'chu talkin' 'bout? I'm a grown ass man. If my mama don't like something, she's welcome to carry her ass home. This my house."

She fidgeted slightly. I could see that I would have to put my mama in her place. Although we'd just made up a week ago, I didn't mind having all that shit come tumbling down all over again. She was being nice nasty without cause, and I wasn't gon' tolerate that shit.

"Come here," I said to Kenya as I sat on the bed.

She came close, so I put my hands at her waist, pulling her between my legs. "Just like you're proving to me that I'm a priority to you, I'm gonna prove that shit to you. My mama don't run shit here but what I allow her to run. Now that you're here, she needs to go run her own shit. I don't mind making that shit known. You my number one too, and I truly feel like you're my one, period. She's not gonna come between that."

Kenya slid her arms around me and lowered her lips to mine, then rested her forehead against mine. I could feel her take a deep breath. I slid my hands to her face and gently caressed her cheeks. "Talk to me, baby. Tell me what's bothering you."

"I... I just don't want to cause drama between you and your mother. I'll never be cool with being in the middle of that."

I pulled away from her. "Look at me, Kenya." When she lifted her eyes to mine, I continued. "You won't be in the middle, but if she can't respect your presence in my life, me and her gon' have a problem. You mean so much to me in such a short amount of time. She not finna fuck with destiny. Walk boldly in her presence. You hear me?"

She nodded, but I knew my mama and I would be having a come to Jesus meeting before it was all said and done.

"Y'ALL ARE ALL OVER THE FUCKING PLACE. ONE MINUTE, I'M threatening you to shoot your shot, and now y'all damn near married. What the fuck?" RJ ranted.

I slowly shook my head as he and Noah laughed. I was glad they were in good spirits. Noah had said that he'd sensed this was coming with his grandfather a while ago. When he got inducted into the Rock-N-Roll Hall of Fame, his grandfather seemed extremely emotional and sentimental. That wasn't like him. He said that he missed his wife, and hopefully, they were together again.

When I asked what he meant by that and why he didn't know if his grandmother was in heaven or not, he said that she was so evil sometimes, she could have busted hell wide open. I was literally frozen for a minute when he said it. He was so serious too. I'd never heard him speak negatively about anyone except that dude that was fucking with him about his ex-wife. When he talked about the negative things about my father, it wasn't in a hateful manner, just matter-of-factly. The way he spoke of his grandmother was somewhat malicious.

He didn't dwell on it though. He quickly brought the conversation back to Kenya and me. When we'd walked through the door, he and RJ were all in our shit, especially when Kenya kissed me and walked off to go chill in the kitchen with TAZ and Raqui. We were holding hands and behaving like we'd been together for months, kissing each other every two minutes it seemed.

I slowly shook my head as they continued to laugh. "Don't hate on what we got, nigga. We grown grown and know what we want."

"Shiiiid, I ain't hatin'. Nigga, I'm in awe. I had too much shit going on in my life to move that damn fast. But hey, you like it, I love it. You definitely gotta be kin to Noah. That nigga move fast as hell too."

Noah rolled his eyes. "Grandpa used to stay on my ass about that shit too. One time, when I was a teenager, he asked if I was having sex. When I told him no, he was like, and you still wanna move that fast?"

"Grandpa couldn't understand your speed if you hadn't sampled the goods yet," RJ said, then laughed.

I slid my hand over my face. I'd definitely sampled the goods… a few times now. After my mama left that night, I stayed putting my hands in places they shouldn't have been, begging for a taste. She finally gave in about midnight. I felt totally fine, but I didn't know how I would feel with extremely strenuous activity.

The first night, Kenya rode me the whole time. I wasn't in the least bit complaining. The way she bounced on my dick had my toes curling and my eyes rolling to the back of my head, feeling like a whole bitch. The woman had skills. She said that she hadn't slept with her ex in an entire month. From that admission alone, she should have known he was sleeping with someone else. Her pussy was way too good to ignore.

I told her that she was extremely trusting, but she told me that she refused to check after a grown ass man. If he was fucking up, it would come to light sooner or later. She refused to stress herself out, worrying over a man that should know what he wanted. She also quoted her favorite lines. *I'm almost forty years old. I'm too old for that bullshit.* When she said it, I rolled my eyes. We had only been together a few days, and I'd heard it more times than I could count.

Monday and yesterday, I'd fucked her every way known to man, all over my house—against the wall, in the shower, on the dinner table, and on the stairs. I even slid into her while she was taking cornbread from the oven. I couldn't get enough. Her screams of passion were sexy as fuck. That alone had me busting prematurely. If we weren't sleeping or eating, my dick was in her walls, wanting to repaint them every chance I got.

My mama had come over to see about me Tuesday evening and almost got an eyeful. Had I not looked up at the monitor to see her coming in, she would have seen me pinning Kenya against the laundry room door, wearing her pussy out. I didn't know why she used her key when she knew I had company. Before I could address it, she apologized, saying she forgot.

That talk was going to have to come sooner rather than later, because she barely said two words to Kenya the entire hour she was there. She didn't have a problem talking to Kenya when we were in Baltimore. It was just now that she saw how serious we were, she wanted to be on guard for bullshit. Had I not gotten injured, Kenya wouldn't have been at my place. We were moving fast as hell, like RJ had said, but I couldn't help it with a woman like her... my cougar.

I chuckled at the thought as RJ stared at me and slowly shook his head. "She done put that shit on his ass. Look at him. Nigga sprung already. Noah, you know a lil something about that, right? Sonya had you chasing her ass for ten years."

He laughed as Noah side-eyed him. "J, shut the fuck up. You try to play hard, but you know Jazzy got that ass on lock."

"Hell yeah, she do. Shorty make me better all the way around. That shit didn't happen that fast though. Look at me now though. I got three successful branches of JC Architectural Firm. I mean, I'm a smart nigga, but shorty add to it. You got me off topic though. We ain't talking about me. We talking about lover boy over there. So, I have a question, Nate. This serious."

I sat up in my seat, waiting for what he would ask. He'd wiped the smile right off my face when he got serious. "How are your feelings for Jessica? Don't be entering into something serious with Kenya if you still hung up on her."

I nodded repeatedly. "I still have feelings for her. I may even still love her, but I'm doing good getting her out of my system. I blocked her on social media. I don't go to her page. She messaged me to see if I was okay. I let Kenya read it and had her reply to Jakari instead. I haven't replied to Jess. I deleted our thread."

"Just be sure, man. RJ is right. Although I was with Jah, I found myself comparing her to Sonya whenever we would have a disagreement. While I know my history with Sonya was way more extensive than your history with Jess, I still feel like you were in way too deep with her. Don't try to replace what you feel for her with Kenya. Let it be something new and totally different. You get what I'm saying?" Noah asked.

"Yeah, I do. I'm thinking about distancing myself from Jakari a bit, too, for right now. That's my boy, and we've gotten close, but whenever I talk to him, I think about her. He only brings her up occasionally, like when she had her baby. Other than that, we don't talk about her. He respects the fact that I'm moving on and even encouraged it, but he's her cousin."

Noah and RJ both nodded. I assumed that meant they agreed with my reasoning. We remained quiet for a moment until I heard Raqui say, "Uh oh. They're quiet. Something must have happened."

Kenya and TAZ both made their way into the room with us as Noah chuckled. When TAZ sat on his lap, he wrapped his arms around her. "Nothing happened, baby. Something thought provoking was said, so we all were thinking about it."

Kenya sat on my lap as well and kissed my lips. "You okay? You need anything, Nate?"

"There's only one thing I need, and I know I'll get that later tonight."

"Not if y'all staying here, you ain't," Noah said as TAZ nudged him.

"Oh, in case you didn't know, Noah is the designated hater around these parts," RJ added with a chuckle.

I slowly shook my head. These niggas around here were nosy as hell. Kenya's cheeks were red, so I kissed her and said, "I'm sorry if I embarrassed you."

"The last thing I am is embarrassed. Let's go to Noah and Taryn's room."

"Like hell!" Noah yelled.

We all burst into laughter, then I wrapped my arms around Kenya. It was good to know that she had a sense of humor. She would have to around us, especially RJ's ass. Noah and RJ would have to suffice as my go-tos when I needed advice, especially relationship advice. I needed a solid brotherhood, one that would help me on my journey with Kenya. I wanted to be everything she needed and more. While I knew I would make mistakes or bad decisions, I also knew that my brothers would help me overcome them.

CHAPTER 12

KENYA

The funeral was a beautiful celebration of Phillip Brooks's life. Noah and his mother had wonderful things to say about him, along with Noah's father, Reverend Ryan Charles. RJ had shocked everyone when he went to the mic to talk. While it was a celebration, it was still emotionally charged until RJ got up there talking about their grandpa. He had everyone laughing so much they could barely breathe, saying that their grandpa was a gangsta.

Leaving Nate was the hardest part. The funeral was on Friday, and we both left Sunday morning. I'd been with him a week, and I had already gotten used to being cuddled under him. Although he was younger than me, the man was perfect. He was so mature for his age. There wasn't a moment where I could see the age difference or that he was being immature. We got along perfectly.

Now that I was back in Chicago, I was miserable. He'd flown back to Dallas to meet with the team doctors on Monday so they could evaluate him again. He'd been evaluated while we were in Houston and in Baltimore, but they needed to be sure that he was ready for practice this week. If I didn't have to go to the studio, I would have asked to go with him to Dallas. However, I realized I was being *too* clingy.

He said he liked that, and since we were still new, his feelings were probably genuine. I didn't want to make that a common practice though. As we progressed, he could get tired of me always wanting to be where he was, crowding him. I told him how clingy I could get, but I didn't know if he truly understood the level of clinginess I was talking about.

I was so happy to be in a relationship with someone that showed me as much attention, care, and love as Nate that I would follow him to the damn bathroom to sit on side the tub while he took a shit. That was disgusting, to say the least, so I forced myself to keep my thoughts to myself and carry my ass back to Chicago. I needed to be with my mama anyway, to make sure she was doing okay with her dialysis.

She had a bad habit of saying everything went well when it really didn't. She'd told me that one day, and I found out from the nurse that they had to pull seven liters of fluid off her. That meant she'd been eating foods she wasn't supposed to and drinking more fluids than she should. She said she didn't want us to worry about her, but she was doing things that caused us to worry.

After I wrapped up my session in the studio, I headed to my place to check my mail. Taryn's house was closer to the airport and the studio, so I'd stayed there. The northside was way away from everything, but I enjoyed the peace and quiet. However, the journey to my place took nearly an hour with all the traffic. By the time I got home and had gone to my box to get the mail, I was exhausted, but the flowers at the door halted me.

I had a restraining order in place. Hopefully, Arik didn't have his ass at my place. I stooped to pick them up and saw the basketball sticker on the envelope. My cheeks heated up. Nate was going to spoil the hell out of me. Before long, I would be expecting to receive a bouquet every week. He must have given instructions for them to leave it at the door, knowing I would be here shortly after.

I unlocked the door and walked inside, holding the mixed bouquet of lilies, tulips, and roses. After setting them on the countertop, I pulled the card from the stem.

Hey, baby. I miss you already. I enjoyed the week we were together, and I can't wait until we're together that way all the time. I know that you're my one, and I'm yours. We fit. Talk to you later. Nate

There was a heart drawn next to his name. I was smiling so big as I picked up my cell phone to text him my thanks. I wasn't sure where he was, so to keep from disturbing him, I sent a text message.

Thank you so much for the flowers. They are beautiful. Our time is coming, and I can't wait either. Call me when you can. I'm done with my session.

I smiled as I sniffed the flowers, then pulled the mail from the bag on my shoulder to go through it. When I saw the letter with Arik's return address on it, I rolled my eyes. My curiosity wouldn't allow me not to open it. I slid the letter opener along the seam and pulled out the letter. It was simpler than I thought it would be.

Kenya,

I'm so sorry. I messed up bad. Can we please talk? I realize the error of my ways, and I just want to have a calm conversation with you. Please call me.

Arik

He was out of his mind if he thought I was going to call him. There was no way in hell. He'd probably seen me with Nate on the internet. When I pulled up my browser and saw the picture of us on the front page, I nearly swallowed my damn tongue. People were talking a lot. I was just glad he didn't really go anywhere with Jessica. I think they may have gone to dinner once, but there was no real media coverage.

I knew the only reason there was coverage about us was because he'd gotten hurt. They were there to get the scoop on his injury but ended up getting the scoop on his personal life. Nate seemed to be happy about it, like he was ready to put our relationship out there. It would have been out there anyway had we been able to go to dinner. That shit happened so fast.

I overheard what he said to RJ our first day in Baltimore. He was distancing himself from his friend because he was Jessica's cousin. For a moment, my mind ran free, thinking that we were moving too fast if he had to take those precautions to ensure he didn't want to reach out to her. However, I decided to look at it as a respect thing, not just for me but for Jessica's man as well.

When my phone began ringing, I smiled big, especially when I saw Nate's name. "Hello?"

"Hey, baby. How was your session?"

"It was good. All went well. I got a phone call from Ledisi's manager. I have to sing background vocals for her show in Chicago next month. They'll be sending me a list of songs to go over and contact information for the other singers as well."

"Damn, baby! That's exciting! I'm happy for you. Do you know the exact date of the concert?"

"Yeah, I do. It will be during the playoffs though. Do you have the game schedule yet?"

"I do. Damn. It's like I hope we are still playing, and then I hope we get eliminated so I can be there for you."

I giggled. "That's okay. We'll both be doing our thing. I'll have support from my mom, and I know you'll have support from your mom."

"If she can make the game. If not, Noah may come. His tour ends in two weeks. He has Los Angeles, Saint Louis, and Baton Rouge left... I think."

"I miss you already too. That week spoiled me just that quickly."

"Yeah, me too. Off season, you gon' get sick of me, girl. I'm gon' be closer to you than your damn shadow."

I laughed. "If I didn't have this studio session scheduled, I would have wanted to go to Dallas with you. How did your appointment go?"

"Man, that would have been nice. My appointment went good. I can practice tomorrow with the team. We have a game in Sacramento day after tomorrow. I might be able to play. If I play, do you think you'll be able to fly out?"

"I would have to do a quick turnaround. I have another session Friday morning, so I would have to leave Thursday. Get me a ticket for tomorrow, baby."

"Hell yeah. My umm... my mom will be there. I think she'll be cool, but let me know if she isn't. I need to have a talk with her anyway."

Shit. "Okay."

"I can hear the disappointment. Don't give up on her yet. I think she sees just how deep this is already. She probably feels like she's gonna lose her baby. That's something that she'll just have to get over though. I'm not letting you go to appease nobody."

My cheeks heated up again. *My man. Shit!* I was on the verge of saying, *Damn, I love you.* Nate was every woman's dream. Before I could respond, a call came in, interrupting our conversation. It was my mother. "Nate, what are you doing?"

"I'm at home, chilling. You have to go?"

"I need to talk to my mama right quick. She's calling. I'll call you back as soon as I get off the phone with her."

"A'ight, baby."

I ended the call and immediately called her back. She answered on the first ring. "Kenya, umm... are you coming here?"

"Yes, ma'am. I was checking my mail. I should be leaving in an hour or so. Is everything okay?"

"Yes, but Arik is sitting on the porch waiting for you."

"Call the police, Ma. I filed a restraining order against him."

"Are you sure?"

"Absolutely. I've already had a conversation with him. He should have said everything he needed to say then."

"Okay. I'm going to ask him to leave. If he doesn't, then I'll call."

"Mama, don't open the door for him. While I don't think he's dangerous, you never know what someone will do out of desperation. He seems desperate to talk to me all of a sudden. I don't like that. I'm going to head your way now."

"Okay, baby."

I ended the call and quickly grabbed my bag. I could check my mail later. My mama needed me. I wanted to call the police anyway. He knew better. I was more than sure he'd gotten a copy of the restraining order. Niggas always wanted to give their all when they knew they'd lost. That shit was toxic as hell. He was only doing this to get me back. If I were to give in, within a month tops, he would go back to his old behaviors.

I'd seen it time and time again in so many relationships. I didn't have time for it. I'd never dipped back to an ex. Once a nigga fucked up with me, that was it. There was nothing he could do to entice me to take him back. I didn't play those kinds of games.

When I got to my car, I called Nate. "Hey, baby," he said as soon as he answered the call.

"Hey. Arik is at my mother's house. I told her to call the police, but I'm going over there."

"Promise me that if he's still there, you won't get out the car, Kenya. Wait for the police."

"I will, but I'm so pissed. Like, how dare he? Suddenly, he has all this fucking time that he didn't have when we were together. He was too busy giving it to another woman. But I'm supposed to forgive him for that shit and take him back? He got me fucked up."

Nate was completely quiet as I ranted, letting me get everything out of me. Once I was finished talking, I honestly felt better... more at ease. Maybe I needed to get all that out. After it was quiet for a minute or so, he said, "How do you feel now?"

"Better. Thank you. I'm sorry."

"You don't have to apologize. You think he saw us on the internet?"

"That's possible. Plus, I don't think I put my mama's address on the damn restraining order. I think I only put my address and Taryn's. Shit!"

"Can you update it?"

"I think so. I'll have to call the police out to my mama's house, I suppose. Nate?"

"What's up, baby?"

"Why are you so damn perfect?"

He chuckled. "I'm not perfect, Kenya, but maybe I'm perfect for you. I feel like you're perfect for me. Our chemistry is so strong, and there isn't an ounce of hesitancy when we're near one another. That's that grown woman shit. I love that."

I assumed he'd been dealing with indecisive women. "Am I the only woman you've dated that was older than you?"

"You mean a woman that was damn near forty years old?"

I rolled my eyes and chuckled. "You make me sick!"

"Well, I mean, that's how you normally say it. But yeah. I feel like a year or two doesn't count, but I would say seven years does. So you're my first and my last."

I felt like my breath got caught in my throat. The shit he said always had the same effect on me. He was so confident in us. It was refreshing, honestly. "Are you saying that if we don't work out, you'll never date an older woman?" I asked to fuck with him.

"Don't play with me, Kenya. I can hear the smile in your voice. You it for me, baby," he said tenderly.

That shit nearly yanked the tears from me. "Damn, Nate. You say some of the most beautiful shit."

He chuckled. "I'm sure about us. I've never been so sure about anyone."

"I'm sure about us too."

"Baby, I have to take a call. It's my agent. I'll text you when I'm free, in case you're still at your mother's house."

"Okay, Nate. Talk to you later."

He was right. He was going to be it for me. His confidence was definitely infectious. I was smiling while stuck in traffic. That shit had to count for something.

"How long ago did he leave, Ma?"

"About thirty minutes ago. He went to his car and just sat there, like he was trying to wait for you to get here. What's going on with him? He seemed a little nervous."

"I have no idea. When I was his, he hardly ever wanted to spend time with me. He always had somewhere to go that I couldn't accompany him to. He found every reason he could to be away from me. Now that someone else has my attention, there's a problem."

"Yeah. You and Nate are trending. I just want you to know that the two of you look amazing together. That picture of you kissing him while standing in that chair looked so passionate. To say y'all have only been a couple for a week, there's more passion between the two of you that some people don't ever see in a relationship. It's beautiful, and it reminds me of how your father and I were when we met in college."

My dad had been deceased for thirty-five years, and my mother still held a sadness inside of her. She wasn't able to get closure, because he committed suicide. While he'd left us four years prior to that, she knew it was his illness causing those erratic behaviors. She tried her best to get him help, but because of the musical genius he was, the music industry used him, ignoring the torment that had surfaced from the inside. As long as he was still producing quality music, they didn't care.

It made my dad feel like there was nothing wrong with him, since my mother was the only one saying anything about it. They argued all the time. I just wished I would have had more time with him, because I had no memories to call my own. Taryn didn't remember him either, because when he left, he never came back to even see us. She has fleeting memories of moments with him, but none of what he was like as a father.

I gently rubbed my mama's back as she gave me a tight smile. Sitting next to her, I pulled her in my arms. She kissed my cheek and said, "I'm okay, baby. I'm just happy for you. This seems like the real deal, even though you got you a youngin."

I chuckled. Before I could respond, there was a loud knock at the door. I already knew that Arik had come back. I immediately called the police, letting them know of my restraining order and how I needed to add my mother's address to it. He wasn't in violation of it if I wasn't here without her address being listed.

They assured me that they would be here momentarily. Arik continued to bang on the door, but what caused me to stand was when he said, "Kenya! I have information for you about your father! Please come to the door!"

My mama stood next to me. "Did he say what I think he said?"

"Yes, ma'am. I still don't want to open the door."

Instead, I went to the door and asked, "What kind of information?"

"The industry owes y'all a ton of money. They've been keeping royalties from his music and only sending y'all pennies. I have a friend who is fascinated with your father's career, and he's been researching him for years. He uncovered so much… even about the night he died."

I looked at my mother, both of our eyes wide. "I called the police, Arik. So you need to leave. Meet me at Lulu Belle's tomorrow morning, if you can, at eight."

"Okay. See you then. Please unblock my number."

As I glanced out of the window, I could see him running to his car. He peeled out, and I turned to my mama. "We have to call Taryn. Are you going to come with me in the morning to meet with him?"

"Absolutely. I thought our attorney had done a good job, getting us what was rightfully ours. The woman he was with when he committed suicide wasn't his wife. Legally, I was still his wife. I refused to even file for divorce, because I knew he wasn't in his right mind. He refused to take his meds because he said it stifled his creativity somewhat. I didn't see or hear a difference. The only thing I noticed was that it was causing him to gain weight."

I nodded in agreement. This was some shit. I was thankful Arik had risked his freedom to come find me to tell me about it, although he could have mailed it like he did that other pitiful letter. I pulled my phone from my pocket and called Taryn to tell her what he'd said, and she assured me she would be on the next thing smoking to Chicago. She needed to be here for the meeting in the morning, then she would get a flight out the same day.

Maybe my time with Arik was worth more than I thought. We were supposed to meet and have a relationship for this very reason. While I had my phone in my hand, I sent Nate a text message. *Hey, baby. I have a lot going on. It will be later when I can call.*

There was a knock at the door, so I went to it to see Officer Atwater. I opened the door and allowed him and his partner inside to update my restraining order. I just hoped Arik wasn't playing games with me. The police would be arresting me for fucking him up instead of him if he was.

CHAPTER 13

NATE

When I walked into the arena in Sacramento, I didn't feel as great. That shit had nothing to do with my concussion though. I hadn't talked to Kenya since day before yesterday. After I received the text about her calling me later, I didn't hear from her that night. I passed out because I had an early flight to Cali. The first thing I did when I woke up was look at my phone to see if I'd missed her call, and there was nothing.

Yesterday, I still didn't hear from her, and I was worried. She was supposed to be joining me here in Sacramento, but since I hadn't heard from her, I was sure she had missed the flight. I called Noah, and he said Taryn had flown out to Chicago the night before. That only increased my nerves.

When he told me what was going on and the reason her ex had gone to her mother's house, I felt for Kenya and just wanted her to reach out and let me know that she was okay. I tried to give her space because of what was going on with her yesterday, but here it was, after four in the evening, west coast time, and I hadn't heard a peep.

I grabbed my phone and sent a text to her. *Kenya, baby, please don't shut me out. I know you are going through a lot right now, but please let me know that you are okay. I'm worried, baby.*

Right after I hit send, a text came through from her. I supposed she was texting me as I texted her. I breathed out a sigh of relief.

Hi, Nate. I'm so sorry for my silence. It seems that I'm grieving the loss of a father I don't even remember. With all the information we were given regarding the record company and the shit that happened to my dad, there is speculation about whether he committed suicide at all. He could have been murdered, since he'd been in a heated argument with someone that night. I'm so sorry I shut you out. That wasn't my intent. I lay in bed all day yesterday with my mama, consoling her and trying to keep it together for her, only to come undone later.

It's so much to handle, and we're in the process of hiring an attorney to take our case with the information we've been given. I was in the studio this morning and practically all afternoon with the other background singers for the Ledisi gig next month. I miss you, and I just want to lay in your arms, letting you console me in only a way you can. Call me after the game. I'll be watching. Are you playing?

I lowered the phone for a moment, thankful that she was feeling my absence as much as I was feeling hers. My mind was starting to take me through all the negative possibilities about moving so fast. Jessica had even crossed my mind, thinking Kenya was going back to her ex and going to hurt me the same way Jess did. It seemed I was suffering heartbreak, because I gave too much too soon to the wrong people.

Lifting my phone again, I responded. *Thank God you're okay. I'm not playing tonight. I was so worried I gave myself a headache, and I knew I wouldn't be focused on the game without hearing from you. Thank you for reaching out. I'm so sorry for what you're going though about your dad. Is it okay if I fly out to meet you in the morning? I have a three-day break before the next game.*

I'm so sorry I stressed you out, Nate. You can absolutely come to me. I can't wait to see you.

I took a deep breath and closed my eyes as my phone vibrated again in my hand. It was a message from Noah. *Hey, bruh. Have a good game tonight. Let me know what your schedule is like two weeks from now. I'd like to take you to visit your grandfather in H-Town. We can go right after my Baton Rouge show.*

I'd have to get back with him later on that. By then, we would be in the playoffs. We only had this game and another game before the post season started. I responded, *I'll let you know for sure tomorrow.*

He responded immediately, but I didn't open it, just so I would remember to respond tomorrow. As I made my way to the arena, a couple of people stopped me and wished me well. I was thankful for the love I received from players as well as coaches and execs. My mind drifted back to Kenya and what she was going through. I was prepared to hear my mother's mouth when she didn't show up to sit with her.

I would have to defend Kenya, and that would also be a perfect time to talk to my mama about her behavior when Kenya was with me a week ago. After I sat, several kids came up to me for autographs, and I obliged them. I didn't have to be here this early since I wasn't playing. Honestly, I didn't have to be here at all, but it wasn't like me to not be here, rooting for my teammates.

I'd gotten injured before about three years ago, not long after I had made it to the pros. It was only a broken finger, so I showed up to all the games until I could play again. That proved my loyalty and devotion to my team. That would serve me in the long run when it would come time to negotiate my contract. Although I wasn't the superstar, I was a vital part of our young team. They looked up to me and had all nominated me to be the team captain, despite LeClaren's stardom.

He was a humble guy. He was cool with me being the captain. Leading our team to victory was all that mattered to him. He averaged forty points a game. We were the Michael and Scotty duo for our team. People actually referred to us in that way. One announcer had compared us to Shaq and Kobe but without all the drama. I could only chuckle. Our dynamic was nothing like that. I knew my role. I wasn't trying to be the team's franchised player.

I went back to Kenya's message and replied. *I can't wait to see you either. I'll call you after the game.*

I went to my phone and booked a flight for early tomorrow morning. She and I would have to have a talk about my expectations in our relationship. I wasn't cool with her going silent, not with me. I should be the one person she wanted to talk to, even if it was a simple text saying she was okay.

"Do you think it's wise for you to be so caught up with this woman? She didn't show up to your game after you bought her a plane ticket. That was a waste of money, Nate. Are you sure she isn't using you or just with you for who you are in the sports world?"

My mama had come to my room when I texted her to tell her about my flight to Chicago. I figured I would be gone by the time she saw it. I didn't get to talk to her last night after the game. One of her friends had met her there, and they had gone out to dinner. I was out for the count by the time she got in last night.

"Ma, her sister is TAZ. Her brother-in-law is Noah. She has a career in music. Being with me wouldn't benefit her at all."

"Yes, it would, son. It would give her more attention. Unless she got in some sort of trouble, the media wouldn't be interested in her. However, being with you would put a spotlight on her. People would start researching her to see who she was. I just don't want you to get hurt, baby."

"Listen. I'm close to thirty-three years old, Ma. I don't need you acting like a jealous ex-girlfriend when I bring a woman around. It's been me and you for a long time, so I understand. However, my heart is attaching itself to Kenya. I feel like she's genuine, and I need you to respect her as the woman in my life. None of that nice nasty shit you did last weekend. She's a nice woman and didn't deserve your shadiness. Believe me, she sensed it."

"So, she talked to you about me? That could be her trying to kick me off the scene."

"No one can alienate you but you when it comes to me. I need you to respect my decisions as a grown man. She offered to leave to make you more comfortable. I insisted that she stayed. She's a good woman, and she needs me right now... emotionally. She's going through some things, dealing with her father's estate, which is another thing that would offer her plenty of attention. She's the daughter of a renowned singer, musician, and musical genius. So, if I'm gonna fall flat on my face, let me. It won't be the first time. I have to explore our chemistry. I feel like Kenya is the one for me, and as long as she is respectful to you, I expect you to be on board. If not, it will be your loss."

Her eyebrows lifted. "You would kick me to the curb. You *would* be alienating me, Nate."

"Again, you would be alienating yourself by not honoring my wishes. I can handle my own romantic affairs. If I need advice, I'll ask for it. Because of your behavior, unsolicited advice is unacceptable. It proves you don't have my best interest at heart... only your own. I love you, Ma. I want you in my life. Real shit. I'm standing firm on this though, just like I did about my father. This is my life. You've lived yours, so let me live mine."

She nodded repeatedly. I could tell by her downturned lips that she was offended, but she had no one to blame but herself. She'd put herself in that position by minding my romantic business. I needed her to respect me as a man. She wanted to continue looking at me and treating me as her little boy. I was so far removed from that shit.

I totally understood why she was doing the things she was doing. However, I needed her to understand how toxic that shit was. She needed a man to claim her attention. I would never tell her that, because I knew she wouldn't handle that advice well coming from me. Hopefully, someone else close could enlighten her. I didn't want there to be another hiatus in our relationship, but I needed Kenya, and I knew she needed me. I refused to let anyone come between what we had.

I grabbed my luggage and made my way to the hotel room door when my mama said, "Fine, Nate. I'll back off. I love you, and I truly want you to be happy. Time will tell if I'm wrong about her. For your sake, I hope I am. Call me when you land."

She walked over to me and kissed my cheek, then left the room before me. I left as well, heading to the lobby to wait for my car. Reporters were everywhere, and I regretted my decision to come down early. I was sure it was because they knew this was the hotel the team was staying in. I did my best to stay out of sight until I received notification my ride was here.

The minute I made my way through the lobby, the vultures collapsed the space around me, bombarding me with questions. One caught my attention when he asked, "Is TAZ's sister, Kenya Zenith, your new love interest?"

I bit my bottom lip, trying to hold in my smile, then turned to him and responded, "Yeah, she is. She's beautiful, huh?"

He chuckled and said, "Absolutely stunning. Good luck."

I nodded at him and made my way to the car amidst the many questions being hurled at me about the game. We'd won last night, but I didn't participate in the festivities with LeClaren and our coach afterward with the media. Since I didn't play, I didn't see a need to. Once I was in my car and we'd taken off, I decided to call Noah.

"Hello?"

"What's up, bruh?"

"Congratulations on the win last night."

"Thanks. I really can't give you a definite answer about my schedule. It'll be postseason. So my schedule all depends on if we win. In two weeks, we'll be in the first round. Can we play it by ear?"

"Absolutely. We can discuss it when it gets closer to that time. I won't tell Grandpa Guillory anything until we know for sure."

"Okay. So how are you holding up?"

"Good. Better than I thought I would."

"I never got to tell you thank you for what you did at the concert. Is there a way I can get a copy of it?"

"Yeah. I'll get my assistant to send it to you. You headed to Chi-Town?"

"Thanks. Yeah, I'm on my way to the airport now."

"A'ight, dude. Be careful."

"Will do."

I ended the call and checked the time to see it was five in the morning. My flight was to leave out at six thirty. While it was extremely early for me, I knew that Kenya was probably awake. It was seven there. We talked briefly last night, and I could hear the sadness in her voice. I just hoped I could help make it easier for her to bear. If I could, I would bear it for her. I sent her a text, letting her know I was headed to the airport.

She responded that she would see me when I arrived, but then she called. "Hello?"

"I just needed to hear your voice," she practically whispered.

"Were you asleep?"

"No. But these are the first words I've spoken. I'm a little hoarse. I guess I overused my instrument yesterday. What time will you land again?"

"The itinerary says twelve thirty-five your time. It's a four-hour flight. I can't wait to get there and hold you, baby."

"I can't wait either. Congratulations on the win last night. I wish I would have made it there. I'm sorry for wasting your money. I have a reimbursement for you."

"That's not necessary."

"Yes, it is. I never want you to think I'm taking advantage of you. Please... let me pay you back."

I didn't respond to her. There was no way I was taking money from her. "Well, get some more rest until I get there. You sound tired."

"I am, a little. I'm gonna go get a medicine ball from Starbucks and some mint tea to keep my throat right."

"When do you practice again?"

"We aren't practicing again until Monday, so you have all of me while you're here."

"Good. I plan to take advantage of every moment. Get some rest, and I'll see you soon."

"Okay. Bye."

I ended the call with my heart heavy. Feeling her sadness and depression was weighing on me. The way she sounded was something I'd never heard from her. Every time I was around her, she was always happy. She didn't sound this bad when she found out her ex was cheating on her.

My soul felt hers. My spirit was intertwined with hers. There was no way I could let my fears or my mother's words interfere with what we had. We just needed to come to an understanding about communication. My heart was already in this, despite my mind trying to warn it to slow down.

I knew without a shadow of a doubt that I was her one and she was mine.

CHAPTER 14

KENYA

My mind was everywhere, and for a couple of days, I thought I'd inherited my father's mental illness of schizophrenia. I didn't feel like myself. When Arik provided documents that uncovered so much wrongdoing concerning my father, I wanted to literally go to Big Easy Records and blow that shit up. Taryn was so torn up inside. Her voice was more like my father's, and it was like she carried him in her soul because of that. Whenever she was feeling a way, she hummed. I believed that was her way of self-soothing.

I wanted to make an appointment with a therapist just to talk things out. My father's death seemed to be wanted by the industry, because he was threatening to uncover so much. There was no proof of what happened to him, only that it seemed he jumped from the window of a five-story building. With all the shit he was stirring, it was speculated that someone had pushed him.

Seeing how the record label was scamming from the beginning, regarding his career, was a heavy blow to all three of us. I literally fell on Arik, crying my eyes out. Then I felt guilty about that, because Nate should have been the only man that I allowed to comfort me. I no longer loved Arik. It was just the situation that had me feeling so emotional. It was like my father's legacy meant nothing to them.

Arik assured me that he respected my decision to leave well enough alone, and he could see that I was happy with Nate. He wasn't typically a shit starter, but he knew what he lost when I left him. He would have been a fool not to at least try to get me back. He even admitted that he'd been too aggressive in his attempts and apologized for everything. Too bad he couldn't show that much effort when we were in a relationship.

After cleaning myself up and straightening my house, I went to the store to be sure I had stuff for us to eat and went to get a medicine ball. By the time I unloaded the groceries and put them in their proper place, it was time to go get Nate. Although I was feeling somewhat down about all the shit that was uncovered the other day, I was excited to see him at the same time. It felt like we'd been a couple forever, and it had only been a little over a week.

I was so remorseful for how I shut him out. It surely wasn't intentional. The information Arik provided us with just took me low, and I didn't know how to handle it. I'd been handling disappointments and failures all by myself for years, even when I was in relationships. I supposed it was habit. I was just grateful that he somewhat understood what I was going through.

When I parked, I saw Nate exit the airport. People were staring, like they were trying to figure out who he was. I quickly got out of my car and waved him over. When he saw me, a big smile emerged on his face. His long strides became quicker, and he got to me in no time. He released his luggage and picked me up, kissing my lips. Although short, it was passion-filled. I loved his kisses and couldn't wait to continue to feel them until he had to leave. "Hey, Nate."

"Hey, baby. You look good."

"So do you," I said as I popped my trunk for him to put his luggage inside.

He came to my door and opened it for me, then walked around to the passenger side. Once he got in, he leaned over and kissed me again. I quickly merged into traffic as he stared at me. "Damn, girl. You look good as hell."

My cheeks heated as a smile played on my lips. I wore leggings with a thin, off-the-shoulder sweater. He softly slid his finger over my bare shoulder as a chill went up my spine. "Thanks, Nate."

I concentrated on getting out of O'Hare airport, fighting the traffic. Maneuvering through this traffic was some shit I could do without in my life. Once we were on the highway, I reached over and grabbed his hand. "I'm so sorry about shutting you out. I realized it was somewhat of a habit. I tend to handle problems on my own, even when I had a boyfriend. I didn't even think twice about it."

"Well, from now on, I need you to think about it. What am I here for? If I'm your man, why wouldn't you lean on me? Forget about those past niggas. They obviously didn't know how to cherish their woman. I promise you, I know how to take care of you from the inside out. I don't miss shit when it comes to my woman. I need you to lean on me. Show me you need my attention and the consolation I can provide. That's what real niggas do, baby."

I nodded, thankful that I chose to reach out when I did. "You're so perfect and so for me. Lord, have mercy."

"Always remember to depend on me to be there for you. When you're hurting, disappointed, sad, pissed, whatever. I want your first thought to be about your one... the man that's perfect for you... Nate Guillory. Period. I'll drop everything for you. I have enough money to live well, even if I don't play another game in the NBA. I feel that strongly about you already, Kenya. Take advantage of that shit."

He slid the backs of his fingers over my cheek as I heated from his touch. I didn't know what I did to deserve a man like him, but I was thankful. I glanced at him and gave him a small smile. "I promise I'll do better. Again, I'm so sorry, baby."

"A'ight. I forgive you. You don't have to keep apologizing. Just so you know, I put Sheila in her place this morning. When she started talking shit about you not being there, I had to politely tell her to mind her fucking business and let me mind mine."

My eyebrows lifted as he chuckled. "I said politely, woman. I didn't talk to my mama like that. I just said that I was grown, and I can handle my romantic affairs without her interference."

"That sounded so much better."

He laughed, causing me to laugh as well. He grabbed my hand and gently caressed it between his large ones, then asked, "So where are we headed?"

"To my place to put your luggage down. My mama wanted to see you, so I told her we would come by. She's supposed to be cooking to welcome you to Chi-Town."

"Hell yeah, 'cause I'm starving. I only had a blueberry muffin and coffee for breakfast."

"You can get a bag of chips from my house or some other snack to hold you over in case she isn't done."

"A'ight. Hopefully, I won't choose to have another snack and end up hungrier."

I frowned until I glanced at him and saw him licking his lips as he scanned my body. "Mm. Well, you won't hear any objections from me, baby."

Just that quickly, I was gushy. I was turned on the minute I laid eyes on him, but him insinuating a good time had me on overflow. He slid his hand to my thigh and gripped it, causing a tremble to go through my body. This young nigga had turned me the hell out.

———

"NATE! IT'S SO GOOD TO SEE YOU, BABY. HOW HAVE YOU BEEN SINCE your concussion?"

"I've been good, thanks to your daughter taking care of me." Nate went to Mama and gave her a hug as she blushed. "Now, what you cooking in here? It smells good!"

I twisted my lips to the side as I watched my mama gush over Nate's fine ass. I rolled my eyes as my mama said, "Baby, I did some smothered turkey wings, pinto beans, cornbread, cabbage, and potato salad."

"All that for me? Shiiiid, I'm in love."

My mama laughed so hard her entire face was red. I rolled my eyes as I shook my head. "Kenya, don't be hatin' on my second mama. She gon' spoil me, huh?"

"Hell yeah," I said. "Just like she spoils Noah."

Out of Taryn and me, I was closest to my mama. Taryn was always on the road as TAZ, trying to make a name for herself, and I was at home with Mama, making sure she was good after her dialysis. Since I was a nurse, it benefitted her for me to be the one to see after her anyway. I didn't fault Taryn one bit for chasing her dreams. She did that shit, and when she made it, she took care of us. That was why I was able to quit my job and become a background singer.

"Noah is the son I never had, and I believe Nate will be my son as well. You remind me so much of Noah anyway. Not in the looks department, but your personality. You're so humble and down to earth. I appreciate that. I hate to bring up Kenya's ex, but that negro was so uppity it was ridiculous. Had I cooked this meal for him, he would have declined a plate."

"Mama Eunice, I'm from Houston. This is how we get 'dine' all the time. I wish I would turn down this food." He hugged her, then said, "Let me go love on Kenya before she starts throwing a fit."

I laughed sarcastically as Nate made his way to me and lifted me in his arms. "You know it's possible for me to shower both of you with attention, right, baby?"

I chuckled as I nodded then kissed his lips. Honestly, I was beyond happy that he and my mama were getting along so well. They'd spent time together whenever we all were in Baltimore, but not enough time to really establish a bond like they were forming now over this food. He lowered me to my feet, being sure to allow my body to slide against his.

We didn't get that snack in before coming here, because I told him I needed a full-course meal. *Fuck a snack.* It had been a week, and I needed our first time reconnecting to be explosive. I needed that shit to feed me physically and emotionally. "Don't start no shit, Nate."

"Oh, I'm starting shit? I'm getting you ready for the festivities after our nap."

"Nap?"

"Hell yeah. You see all this food your mama cooking? Ain't no way I'm gon' be able to stay awake after eating all that. Plus, I'm gon' be too full to do anything anyway, and so will you. We won't have a choice but to sleep that off."

I slowly shook my head then grabbed his hand and led him to the front room to have a seat while my mama glanced at us with a smile on her face. She was so happy that Taryn and I were happy. Although my relationship with Nate was extremely fresh, she felt the intensity of it, just like I did.

Once we sat, his phone chimed. He pulled it from his pocket and glanced at it, then slid it back into his pocket. "That's your brother-in-law. I'll call him later."

He leaned over and kissed my head then put his arm around me. I snuggled against him and took a deep breath. "I hate that we are going to have to open this case against the record label. Not because of my feelings but because of my mama's. I realized the other day that she was still hurting about my father's death. It's been thirty-five years, but she is still grieving him. She didn't get the closure she needed. Although they weren't together at the time, she still loved him."

"I hate that for y'all, too, but at least y'all will have what's rightfully yours, plus some, since they were keeping it from y'all. Evilness never wins in the end. Hurtful secrets, shadiness, and underhandedness have a way of coming to light. How did your ex find out about all of that?"

"He has a friend that has been researching my daddy's brilliance. He loves my dad. Plus, I found out that he worked for the label at some point. Nate…"

I sat up and angled my body to where I could stare into his eyes. "I was so torn up about everything Arik revealed to us, I fell on him, crying my eyes out. I felt so guilty afterward, although I don't have an ounce of love for the man inside of me. I'm sorry."

Nate looked away for a moment. Maybe that was something I should've kept to myself. He grabbed my hand as he nodded. "It's okay. He was there and the one giving you the information. I understand it was the situation. I just wish you would have allowed me a chance to console you."

I felt worse. I lowered my head, feeling disgusted with myself. We sat there quietly for a moment as I thought about how I would feel if I knew Jessica was consoling him in some sort of way. I should've kept my big mouth closed. I just didn't want to feel like I was keeping something from him. With his fingers under my chin, he lifted my head and stared into my eyes.

"It's okay. Thank you for telling me. I just hope this doesn't make him think you're sensitive to him again."

"No. He apologized for his aggressive tactics of trying to get me back, then wished me the best with you. I suppose he saw us online like everyone else."

"Don't worry, Kenya. I'm cool. It stings a bit, but I understand the situation, and I know it wasn't done maliciously or even intentionally."

"It wasn't. I was sitting next to him, and it just happened. How can I make this better?"

"I can think of a few ways. After I eat, I'll fill you in." He stood and made his way back to the kitchen. "Mama, you need some help?"

I was such an ass. *Damn it.* All I could think about was what if Arik was lying and decided to throw that in his face, spinning it like there was still something between us. *Ugh!* Then the validity of my word would have been doubted because I didn't say something first. Hopefully, it would be as easy for him to get passed as he made it seem.

"SWALLOW IT, KENYA. TAKE THIS DICK," HE SAID AS I FOUGHT FOR MY fucking life.

His dick was destroying my fucking esophagus and forcing me to take it like it was nothing. The tears were streaming down my face, but I was still trying to put in work. Tender Nate was gone for now. He was inflicting his punishment on me for shutting him out and allowing Arik to console me. Although he didn't say so, it felt like that was what this was.

His eyes were closed, his lips were tucked inside his mouth, and his head was tilted back as he held my face in his hands. When he opened his eyes and lowered his head, he slowly pulled out of my mouth and gently wiped my tears, making me abandon my previous thoughts. "I'm sorry. I got carried away. Your mouth is so fucking amazing."

He pulled me up from my knees, cradling me to him like a baby, and kissed my forehead, showing me the tenderness I desperately needed. "You forgive me, baby?"

"Yes."

We stayed at my mama's house for nearly four hours. Nate and Mama had a great time, getting to know one another better, and I had an amazing time watching them bond. When we got back to my place, we took an hour-long nap. Well, I would have slept longer had Nate not woke me up with kisses to various spots on my face. We'd fallen asleep on the couch with me lying on top of him, in his arms. That was one of the best feelings in the world.

He walked down the hallway to my bedroom and lowered me to my feet, then lay in my bed. "Come take a seat, baby, so I can take you to ecstasy."

I frowned slightly because I didn't want to just straddle his face if that wasn't what he meant. I hesitantly made my way to the bed as he said, "I promise my beard is soft and comfortable. Once you sit up here, you won't want to get up."

That definitely clarified things for me. I moved a little quicker and straddled his face. He immediately gripped my ass, pulling me to him and began indulging in my fruit like he had a vitamin deficiency. He was taking his time though, allowing his tongue to grace every part of me. I closed my eyes and allowed my head to drop back and subtly rolled my hips against him. I could see how he got carried away earlier, because I was ready to go to the theme park on his ass too. Six Flags didn't have shit on this ride I was on.

I gripped my nipples as I moaned. "Naaaate. Yes, baby."

I swore this man was exposing every sensitive nerve in me. He had me so emotionally open right now. It seemed like he was trying to kill my ass a minute ago, but now he was reminding me of why we were so good together. I already knew that I would fall for him fast as hell. He started a slow rhythm, sucking my clit. My eyes rolled as my legs began trembling.

Nate gripped my ass and pushed his face even deeper into me, causing me to erupt all over his gorgeous face. Before my orgasm could die down, he slid me to his dick, penetrating my core, giving me the very thing I'd been craving. Condoms had seemed to become a thing of the past since our shower session nearly two weeks ago.

Shockingly, I didn't even care. I began rolling my hips as I opened my eyes to stare at him.

"Damn, Kenya. You feel so good, baby."

"You feel good too, Nate."

I flattened my feet on the bed and began a slow bounce on his dick, allowing it to take me away... far away from here. The only thing on my mind was the way Nate had me feeling. His dick comforted all my fears, putting all my doubts to rest. "Naaate... damn. I missed you so much, baby. I'll never go a week without seeing you again. Being without you is painful. All the healing I needed is right here."

"Mmmm. Yeah, Kenya. Let this dick heal you from the inside out."

His moan was so fucking sexy. As his dick continuously slid against my G-spot, I erupted, squirting all over him. He sat up in the bed and held me steady, then began lifting and lowering me on his dick, taking my damn breath away. "Give me all your doubts, insecurities, sorrows, and grief. Let me rid you of all that shit, baby. I'm here for the long haul. Trust me with your deepest emotions. I'm gonna take care of you for the rest of my life. I promise."

For some reason, I believed every word he said. His words consoled me better than I could have ever consoled myself, and his dick made sure that shit stuck. I didn't think he realized just how passionate and powerful his words were. Nate was what every woman longed for in a mate.

He was passionate, considerate, kind, and tender. There were even times that he could be rough... during sex, of course. I didn't need roughness at any other time. I was past that stage in my life. I needed a man that made me feel like I was the only woman for him, like the world revolved around my ass.

Nate made me feel all that and more. He made me feel like it would be impossible for him to even breathe without me. He pulled me down to him and began stroking me from below. I lay on his chest, feeling pleasured, cherished, and even loved as he wrapped his arms around me. I wouldn't fuck up in this manner again. My every action would be influenced by my thoughts of him and his feelings. I couldn't risk losing perfection again.

He tenderly kissed my head as his strokes became a little stronger, forcing the breath out of me. "Damn, Kenya. You feel so fucking good. Our chemistry seems unbelievable."

I moaned in agreement, then lifted my head to kiss his lips. When I did, his strokes got even stronger and slightly faster. My orgasm was on the verge of flooding the area. My entire body had heated up. "Give it to me," he said.

Within seconds, I released all over him. A frown graced his gorgeous face, so I knew he was about to erupt as well. Since he wasn't wearing a condom, he pulled me from it and shot his seed all over my back. No words were spoken after that. Only the sounds of our heavy breathing filled the room for minutes.

After gripping my ass, he said, "I'm glad you're mine. I'm glad this pussy mine too."

I smiled lazily. "I'm glad too. I can't wait to see how much closer we will become."

I assumed he forgot he shot all over my back, because he ran his hands right through it as he caressed me. "Aww shit."

I laughed then grabbed his hand and sucked his fingers clean. The frown on his face as I did so let me know that rough sex was loading, and I would be screaming out my pleasure shortly. I couldn't wait either.

CHAPTER 15

NATE

"**N**igga, what's up? You good?"

"Yeah, I'm cool, J. Sorry I haven't gotten back. Listen…"

"You ain't gotta say. I'm a smart-ass nigga, and I'm a Henderson. We peep shit real quick like."

I huffed. I'd just gotten to my house in Dallas to get ready for the next game. I stayed in Chicago for two days then headed out so I could practice with the team. After this game, the post season would be starting. I also had a doctor's appointment tomorrow morning, to be reevaluated. I was more than sure I would be fully cleared.

Kenya and I had enjoyed our time together. After I got over my pitiful feelings about what she told me, I respected her more for even saying anything. She could have kept that shit to herself. That let me know just how strongly she felt for me if she felt guilty about her ex comforting her during that situation. However, I felt differently about it at first.

I was pissed that she shut me out and let a nigga she had a restraining order out on comfort her. My mind was ready to take me on the same journey it was on before talking to her the day before. We were moving too fast, and she was still hung up on her ex. Jessica had again popped up in my head, not in a way that would make me want to call her but thinking that Kenya was like her. Kenya would go back to him and leave me heartbroken just like she had.

I was glad that I was able to see the bigger picture. Knowing the circumstances, even down to how they were seated, had helped me. He was sitting next to her. She needed comfort from somebody... anybody. He just happened to be the closest to her at that moment.

"J, it's just that whenever I talk to you, I think about her. While I feel like she's leaving my heart, I want to make sure she's completely gone. I spent the past couple of days in Chicago, spending time with Kenya. I wanna love her... even more than I loved Jess." I paused for a moment, then asked, "How is she?"

"I get it, Nate. She's okay. The baby is good too. They are already out and about. She asked about you too. I could tell it bothered her that you didn't respond to her, but I know she understands. I think she still feels guilty about the pain she caused you."

"Well, I'll have to have a talk with her so she can let that shit go. I would rather do that in person, though, so she can see the sincerity in my eyes. Kenya and I are progressing quickly, and I know it will only be a matter of time before I fall for her. Our chemistry is even stronger than the chemistry between me and Jess. Whenever we meet, it'll have to be a public place though, one where Brix and Kenya are there."

"I think I know the perfect time then."

I frowned slightly. "When?"

"We were talking about going to your game."

"Naw. That won't work. Kenya can't be there. She has studio time scheduled."

"Well, did you get the message from Noah?"

I'd completely forgotten about that. I'd been so wrapped up in

Kenya I forgot to check the message. "I did, but I forgot to check it. What's going on?"

"He's giving TAZ a surprise party. He invited all the Hendersons to Baltimore. So you know we going up there country hood style and set that place off."

I chuckled as I thought about their country asses in their boots and shit, fucking up the place with those bad ass kids, not to mention Mayor Storm. "When is it?"

"In two weeks after his tour ends, when y'all will be playing the Wizards. So, you'll be in the area. I believe he took your schedule into consideration."

"Damn. Okay. Kenya didn't say a word about it."

"She may not have known just yet. He said it was sort of last minute."

"Okay."

"Well, it was good talking to you. I'll back off some and let you reach out when you're more comfortable, man. I appreciate you being honest with me."

"Always, man. You've been a good friend to me. Before we go, how's Yendi?"

"She's doing good, and she'll be happy to know that you remembered her name. She's a true fan. We're having a little boy."

"Damn. Congratulations, man. I'm sure you're happy about that."

"I am. I was happy regardless. I'll let you know when the wedding will be. She wants to wait until after the baby is born."

"Okay. Let me know."

"Talk to you later."

"A'ight, man."

I ended the call and sat for a moment. Jess was having a difficult time for a totally different reason. I knew that she was having a tough time, but I thought she was over that, especially when she told me she couldn't talk to me anymore or give me permission to be where she was. So now I knew that was totally for Brixton's benefit.

However, I noticed something different. While my body had heated up slightly when I thought about her, I didn't feel flutters like I used to. She was indeed leaving me, and Kenya was filling all the voids her absence had created. Kenya was so much more than I thought she would be, and I had high expectations. She'd exceeded them all.

After I got settled, I texted her to let her know I was home and would call her a little later. She responded with a simple, *Okay.*

Taking my luggage to my room, I opened it to begin unpacking. When I opened it, there was an envelope right on top. I frowned slightly, trying to figure out when and how it got there. *Kenya.* I opened it to find eight crisp one-hundred-dollar bills and a note. I opened it to read what she had to say, although I had a clue.

Nate,

I am so sorry about the wasted airline ticket. I told you I would reimburse you. I'm pretty sure you'd gotten me a first-class ticket. This is the rate right now. If it costed more, I'll be happy to give you the rest. I appreciate you more than you know. I can't wait to write this type of letter in the future to where I can say how much I love you. However, I feel like that will be coming soon. Talk to you soon.

Kenya

I slowly shook my head, then grabbed my phone and texted, *Kenya...*

There was no way I would keep her money, even if I had to sneak it back to her the way she'd done to me. She didn't respond or call, so I continued unpacking, taking shit to the laundry room to start a load. Afterward, I lay on my oversized sofa to get a nap in. While I was in Chicago, I spent more time in Kenya's pussy than I did sleeping. She was addictive—that was for sure. I knew that I would be flying her to me as soon as possible.

The ringing doorbell woke me up. I was grateful for that because a nigga had been asleep for damn near four hours. I was gonna be up all damn night, now. However, I rarely had visitors here in Dallas. My mama said she wasn't coming until tomorrow, since Dallas wasn't that far. I wiped my eyes and made my way to the door. For a moment, I thought my eyes were deceiving me since I was still groggy. I unlocked the door and flung it open to see my baby standing there.

She smiled big as I scooped her up in my arms. "Kenya! What are you doing here?"

"Well, our session for tomorrow got canceled about an hour after you left, so I got online and got a ticket out. I couldn't miss this game after missing the last one."

I laid my lips on hers, feeling so at peace with her in my arms. I lowered her to her feet and got her luggage to bring inside. "This house is beautiful, Nate. So, I assume you mostly stay here during basketball season."

"Yeah, for the most part. One day, you gon' be staying here during basketball season too."

She blushed so hard. Her cheeks were extremely red. I pulled her close to me, after closing the door, and asked, "Why did they cancel practice?"

"Our chemistry was so good, none of us really saw a need to practice again so soon. They agreed that we would hit it hard two weeks before the show, which will be after... Taryn's surprise party! I saw the message from Noah this morning. I was so wrapped up in you, I never checked my messages."

She giggled, and I chuckled as well. "Same here. I saw it once I got home. I need to talk to you about something. When you mentioned the party, it reminded me."

I saw the concern appear on her face through her lifted and scrunched eyebrows. Once we were seated on the sectional, I pulled her to me. "Jakari called me. Noah invited the Hendersons to the party, so Jessica will be there. I just want you to know that you are the woman I want. Although I was severely caught up with her for a whole damn year, her presence won't threaten a thing. But I need to have a conversation with her."

As I tried to read her expressions, I got confused. Whereas she looked somewhat worried by her facial expression, her demeanor seemed relaxed. I continued. "She's been feeling guilty about breaking my heart. Literally to the point where she overthinks everything. I need to let her know it's okay. Because of what she did, it allowed me to be available for you at a time you needed me. Things happened just the way they were supposed to."

She brought her hand to my cheek and gently caressed it with her thumb. "I trust you, Nate. For a while, I didn't understand how she could choose someone else over you with everything that you had to offer. But I get it now. She wasn't who was meant for you. I was. I supposed God was waiting for us to stop doing our own thing so He could do His work."

My eyebrows lifted as I nodded repeatedly. "I couldn't have worded that any better, baby. Jessica doesn't know that I want to speak with her, but I plan to reach out to her fiancé about it. The last thing I want is confusion. One thing I can pride myself on is keeping the peace where at all possible."

She smiled at me as she gazed into my eyes. "There you go being perfect again. That's very respectful and wise, baby."

"Yeah. In other news, my mama will be here tomorrow. So you will be spending time with her before the game."

"Okay. No worries. I'm respectful too."

She winked as I smiled. "I'm giving you permission to get at her respectfully if she's being disrespectful. That shit she pulled the last time was unacceptable. Put her in her place and put her up on game on where your place is."

"Nate, I don't want any drama with your mother... just like you don't want any with Jessica's man. I'll steer clear of her if she's on that same shit she was on last time."

"How will you steer clear of her if y'all will be riding in the same car? Secondly, I've already discussed the situation with her. If she chooses to do what she wants to do anyway, that means she wants to get her feelings hurt."

"I understand, baby, but I will still leave that task to you. She will never be able to truthfully say that I was disrespectful to her or handled her roughly. I won't do it. I don't even know her well enough for that, and she doesn't know me. She's just trying to protect her baby."

I rolled my eyes and began tickling her. "And there *you* go being perfect."

She hollered in laughter then reached over and grabbed my dick. "Seeeee, you ain't playing fair, baby," I said as I released her and bit my bottom lip.

"All is fair in love and basketball."

I laughed so hard, but then I thought about what she said. I tilted my head as her cheeks reddened for the second time since she'd been here. While I knew she was quoting the movie, I couldn't stop my mind from wandering. Then I thought about her letter. "We're getting there, aren't we?" I asked her.

"Yeah, way quicker than I thought we would. This journey to love with you has been so damn fulfilling. I really just want to be under you every second of the day."

"The feeling is mutual, beautiful. So fucking mutual."

She snuggled against me like she was going to relax for a minute. I frowned as I gently pushed her away from me. She frowned right back, but her frown was one of confusion. "So, you just gon' tease a nigga?

How dare you lead him to think he got action and then forget about him?"

Her eyebrows lifted, and she hollered in laughter as I began tickling her all over again. When I released her, she straddled me. "That wasn't my intent. I'm gonna handle up. I just need a little nourishment first. Can we order something to eat?"

I kissed her lips as I felt my dick harden even more. I could feel her heat through our clothes. "Yeah, but you have to sing to me."

"Sing for food?"

"Mm hmm. Sing and fuck for food."

She playfully rolled her eyes then pulled her shirt over her head and unsnapped her bra. She stood and took her pants and underwear off, then began singing. I was in a fucking trance by her voice and from staring at the masterpiece before me. I loved her body. Her titties were the perfect size, not too big but not too small, although one was slightly bigger than the other, and her ass was thick but proportionate.

I didn't know the song she was singing, but in the chorus of it, she was saying, *I can't get enough, nothing even matters,* and *I want this forever.* As I listened, I slowly pulled my dick from my basketball shorts. When she saw what I was doing, she made her way to me and slid down my dick as she continued singing. I swore that shit sent a chill up my fucking spine. The goosebumps had appeared on my skin as she slowly rolled her hips.

When I saw the tears fall down her cheeks, I pulled her face to mine and kissed everywhere they had fallen. *God, bless it!* She brought her hands to my face as she sang, "On the brink of breaking, even with your love here to stay. Oh, I'll never try, no, I won't deny, your love can't be replaced. I'll keep catering to your will if only to bathe in your grace."

The words to what she was singing sounded familiar, but damn if they weren't hitting me right in the chest, especially when she repeated, *I want this forever.* I gripped her hips as she continued her torturously slow grind. I swore I wanted to tell her I loved her already. I didn't bargain for all this when I made the request. Shit, I would order her a fucking Maserati at this point. To hell with food.

I couldn't take it any longer though. I took control and forcefully grinded her on my shit. She couldn't sing through that shit. Her melodic voice turned into low moans then loud declarations, telling me how I was killing her pussy. I loved when she talked dirty. That shit made my dick even harder, as if that were even possible. Like the song she sang said, I knew I would never get enough.

"Naaate! I'm about to cum all over your nice ass couch!"

I didn't give a fuck about this couch. I'd worry about that shit once we were done. "Give it to me, gorgeous. Fuck all this shit up."

My fingertips dug into her as I gripped her tighter, and she unleashed an unfathomable love all over me... and the couch. I didn't understand how she felt so deeply for me already, but I knew to accept the rareness of it for what it was worth. I didn't understand why I felt so strongly already either. Just as her tremors were dying down, I lifted her and added to the mess. I couldn't wait until I could blast off in her pussy. I could clearly see her having my children, nurturing and loving them.

I rested her on my legs, right in our mess, and said, "Order whatever the fuck you want. You gon' be singing to me all the time now. I hope you know that."

She gave me a soft smile and closed her eyes, threatening to fall asleep sitting up. I chuckled then stood to carry her to the bedroom so we could get cleaned up. I kissed her repeatedly as I carried her up the stairs. When I got to my room, I lowered her to her feet, got a wet towel to wipe the key areas, then went back down for her luggage. I glanced at the couch and slowly shook my head. *Thank God for Scotchgard.*

CHAPTER 16

KENYA

As I looked through the outfit options I'd packed for the game tonight, the doorbell rang. I took a deep breath, knowing it was Nate's mother. He was sure to text her this time, letting her know that I was here. That way there would be no surprises. I hated that he'd already left for an early morning practice. I was hoping she would have arrived either before he left or before he came back home before the game. I wasn't so lucky.

When I opened the door, she gave me a closed-lipped smile and a head nod, then walked in as I stepped aside. "Hello, Ms. Green," I responded.

She could act like an ass if she wanted to. That didn't mean I had to reciprocate. I had done nothing to make her think I wasn't the woman for him other than miss the game the other day, for which I'd reimbursed Nate. Granted, we were shuffling that money back and forth, hiding it in various places, but I was trying to give him his money back. I felt horrible about that.

So, technically, she didn't have a reason to dislike me. She didn't know me. As I was making my way back toward the stairs, she said, "I'm glad you could make it this time."

There her shady ass go. Nice nasty. "Me too. Nate calms my spirit. Finding out all the BS the record label was keeping from us concerning my dad was heartbreaking. It had me immobile with depression for a couple of days."

"Hmph."

That was all she said. I at least expected an 'oh, I'm sorry to hear that' sort of statement from her. I was definitely going to let Nate know how she was behaving. I knew that tight-lipped smile she gave me was fake. Before she knew of my interest in her son, she was cool as ever. Taryn and I had enjoyed getting to know her. She'd flipped the fucking script on me. That was okay though. I would still be with her son, and unfortunately, if she didn't get her issues under control, she wouldn't be in his life.

I truly believed she thought he was bluffing, especially since they'd just made up. She wasn't taking what we had seriously. I knew it seemed so unreal because of how fast it was moving, but it was like neither of us could control it. We were both passionate beings, in search of something real. I'd gone from what I deemed as a frustrated love to embarking on a perfect love.

After turning to make my way to the stairs again, I heard her say under her breath, "Been together two minutes and think that woman gives a damn about him."

I slowed my steps and closed my eyes. After taking a deep breath, I tried to continue, but she came out of the kitchen and saw me. "You okay, Kenya?" she asked way too nicely.

"Yes, ma'am. I have a wonderful man that I look forward to spending the rest of my life with. I couldn't be better."

I walked away, wanting to stomp my way up the stairs. She was pushing me to say something to her ass. I wanted to text Nate so bad. There was no need though. He would sense that shit when he got back home. I was more than sure he would be back in a couple of hours. He said the practice wouldn't be long, and he'd already been gone for two hours.

When I got to his room, I started slinging clothes from my luggage, then stopped and took a deep breath. I couldn't let her irritate me like this. After folding what I wasn't going to wear and laying out the outfit I chose, I closed my suitcase. I still needed to take a shower. After our session on the couch yesterday, I passed out. I slept for an hour, then we ordered food. After eating, we watched a movie then fucked again. We both fell asleep sticky as hell.

I went to the bathroom and started the shower then went to the mirror and pulled my dreads up. After I started my facial, I could see that bitch appear in the mirror, no knock or anything to alert me of her presence. This was getting harder than I thought it would be. She was really trying to push me to curse her ass out. Taryn was the nice one… I wasn't.

"So, what is your angle exactly, Kenya?"

I frowned. "I'm not sure what you mean."

She smiled and rolled her eyes. "I feel like you are only using Nate for what you can get out of him. He falls in love so easily, and women have taken advantage of that. He has a kind heart, and that makes him somewhat gullible and naïve."

"First, Nate approached me. Second, all the attributes you mentioned are the things that attracted me to him. Third, I'm very capable of taking care of myself. I've been doing it my entire adult life. I don't want for anything."

"If you say so. I have my eye on you. It's bad enough you're older than him and probably don't want children now."

"I really don't like how you're assuming you know me. The only thing you know about me personally is my name and, I suppose, my age. You know nothing about my character, so I won't take offense to your accusations since they are ill informed and laced in ignorance."

I turned my back to her and continued my facial while she stood there staring at me like I had cursed her out. "Well, for your sake, I hope I don't have to run interference to keep my son from being heart-broken. I won't be as forgiving as I was last time with Jessica, since I didn't get to meet her."

I rolled my eyes as I rinsed my face then started getting undressed with her standing right there. I didn't give a fuck. She was just miser-able because she had never experienced a man like Nate. His father apparently didn't love her like he loved Noah's mother. She was trash. So, because she was miserable in her love life, she was clinging to her son. She was toxic at best.

I was really praying that Nate showed up and overheard her at first, but the more I thought about it, I was glad he didn't. Tonight would be his first game in over a week. He didn't need to be worried about the bullshit between his mother and me. I was sure she would fix her attitude once he got here. I would pretend that all was well. I wouldn't be overly friendly, but I would respond if she said something to me. If not, I wouldn't have shit to say to her.

I planned to stay in this room as long as possible. If that meant I had to lie down and take a nap, I would. After I took my shower and had dried off, I sat on his bed and moisturized my body. Nate had the most comfortable bed known to man. So, it wouldn't be hard to go back to sleep. After eating a snack from my purse that I'd packed for the flight, I lay in bed, butt ass naked, and went to sleep.

"DAMN, BABY, YOU SMELL GOOD," I HEARD NATE SAY AS HE RUBBED his nose up the back of my neck.

I slowly turned to face him and let a lazy smile grace my lips. "Hey, baby. How was practice?"

"Practice was cool. I was just anxious to get back to you. Have you eaten lunch yet?"

"No. I wanted to wait for you," I said, then kissed his lips.

I glanced at the clock to see I'd been asleep for an hour. That was one hour less that I had to be in his mother's presence. *Bitch.* "So, how did it go with my mother?"

"Fine. We really didn't spend much time together. I was getting my things ready for this evening when she got here. I like to be prepared beforehand. Then, once I finished, last night's festivities caught up with me."

He nodded as if he knew I was withholding the truth from him. He kissed my lips and asked, "So what do you feel like eating?"

"Whatever you want, baby. I'm not terribly picky."

"Okay. Well, I have to be back at the arena in three hours, so I typically like to eat a lot of protein, but not too much to weigh me down and have me feeling sluggish. So I'll probably get some type of chicken and broccoli pasta of some sort or a grilled chicken salad."

"Okay. I'll just eat what you eat."

I kissed his lips again then stood from the bed to put clothes on. "Damn, girl. I didn't know you were naked under there."

I smiled and bit my bottom lip. "Mm. I typically like sleeping naked unless I'm cold or in a hotel room alone. I'm the most comfortable in my birthday suit."

"That's good to know... I mean, for future references. I could have woken you up in other ways."

I grinned at him as I slid on a T-shirt and some terrycloth shorts. He stood from the bed and grabbed my hand. I scooped up my phone from the nightstand and allowed him to lead me downstairs, discreetly taking a deep breath and praying I didn't snap.

When we got to the sectional, his mom was seated there, watching TV. She looked at us and smiled. "Did you sleep well, Kenya?"

"Yes, ma'am. Thank you."

I wanted to add to that, but I was able to restrain myself. When I was about to sit next to Nate, he pulled me down to his lap and cradled me like a baby. He kissed my lips, then turned to his mother to ask if she wanted to order something. She told him what she wanted, then he called the order in. He ended up getting a chicken salad, so of course, I got the same. His mother ordered some type of po' boy. I was doing my very best to tune her out as I relaxed in Nate's arms.

They were having a conversation that I chose not to participate in, and it didn't seem to bother either of them. When the doorbell rang, I stood from Nate's lap so he could go to the door. I could see his mother roll her eyes at me in my peripheral. She could kiss my whole ass. I knew this ride in this car would be interesting as fuck. I'd be sure to bring my AirPods so I didn't have to listen or talk to her.

When the door closed, I made my way to the table, getting to it the same time as Nate. He removed everything from the bag. My eyebrows lifted at the size of the salad. "Oh, wow! It's a lot bigger than I thought!"

Nate chuckled. "Yeah, they *are* pretty big. This is the only size the salads come in though."

"Okay. How much was it so I can give your money to you?"

He frowned hard. I said that shit for his mother's benefit. "Kenya, for real, man. Quit tripping. I'm tired of shuffling that plane ticket money around with you too. I told you to keep that shit. I'm not accepting money from you. Period. You ask again, I'm gon' get real offended."

He sounded offended now. Me trying to make a point to his mother had backfired. I lowered my head and said softly, "I'm sorry."

"Come here," he said somewhat roughly.

I walked to the other side of the table to him as his mother stared at us, seemingly happy that I'd irritated him. When I stood in front of him, he lifted my head by placing his fingers under my chin. After kissing my lips, he said, "Let me be your man, baby. I can take damn good care of you. I've told you that before. Please don't make me have to say it again. Okay? You don't have to prove your independence to me or no one else in this room," he said as he glanced at his mother.

Shit. He knew she was behind my actions. I nodded. "Okay."

I quickly sat in my seat like a scolded child, and he sat next to me. His mother had already dug into her food like we weren't even in the room. "Damn. You couldn't wait for me to bless the food?"

"I'm sorry, baby. I blessed my own. I was starving."

He nodded then grabbed my hand. "Lord, thank You for this meal. Allow it to nourish us as You intended. Take out any impurities that may not be good for our health. Not just out of the food, but out of this house. Allow Kenya to know that no one else's opinion of what we have matters. We know what this is and so do You. Thank You for blessing me with her. She's your angel, and You couldn't have blessed me with better. Amen."

My face was hot as hell as he stared at his mother with a slight scowl on his face. I cleared my throat and dug into my salad without adding dressing. I was so damn nervous. I just wanted to stuff my mouth so I wouldn't say anything else. Nate finally brought his attention to his food, pouring his dressing over it.

I grabbed his fork and attempted to feed him when his mother stood from the table and walked off. He opened his mouth and took it from me. After he finished chewing, I grabbed another forkful to feed him as he stared at me. I was trying to keep his mouth full so we didn't have to talk about it. I didn't want to talk about it before his game, although he was already irritated.

Once he took what I'd extended to him, he took his fork from me. "Eat yours, Kenya. I can feed myself, baby."

I brought my hand to his cheek. I could see the disappointment in his eyes as he stared back at me. His irritation was evident, and I hated this for him. Lowering my hand, I decided to pour the dressing on my salad, and we ate in silence for a while. Once I closed the container it came in, I turned to him and said, "This was so good. Thank you, baby."

"You're welcome."

He'd demolished his. Once he threw the container in the trash and I put mine in the fridge, I grabbed a bottle of water and gave him one too. He grabbed my hand and led me back upstairs. His spirit was so heavy. I could feel it. It had me heavy as well. Once we were inside his room, he removed his shirt and got in bed. I got in bed as well, being sure not to lie down. There was no way I could handle that on a full stomach.

Nate laid his head in my lap, and after a few minutes, he was sound asleep. His mother was pissed. I could see it all over her face before she got up from the table. Nate wasn't a fool by far. He knew what his mother was doing. He probably knew before he even posed the question to me when he first got home. He had cameras all over this house. I wondered if they had sound. If they did, I just hoped he wouldn't be upset that I lied to him. I was only thinking about his mental state for his game.

I played games on my phone while Nate slept, and by the time he woke up, it was time for him to get ready for his ride. He kissed me deeply. When he separated the kiss, I said, "Good luck on your game tonight, baby."

"Thank you. Make sure you come courtside and give me a good luck kiss before the game starts. I'm gonna need it."

I pulled him to me. "Don't think about anything other than playing to the best of your abilities. During those three hours, nothing else matters. You got this, baby."

He nodded and kissed my lips again, then left the room to head to his car. I took a deep breath and prayed for him. His mother meant a lot to him, and I knew he wanted her to be in his life. She'd always been the one there for him. She was being unreasonable, and I truly believed she couldn't help it. It was in her innate nature to be territorial. In her mind, anyone coming into Nate's life, claiming his undivided attention, posed a threat to her position.

That couldn't be further from the truth. His heart was big enough to share. I wished she could see just how much this was hurting him so it wouldn't have to go as far as it did about the issue of his father. She didn't want to share Nate with David. I truly believed that she knew all along who Nate's father was, but because he didn't love her, she didn't want him in the picture, even if that was beneficial for Nate.

I stood from the bed to begin getting dressed. Our car would arrive in two hours to pick us up. We would still arrive at the arena about two hours before the game started. That would give me time to go courtside before Nate disappeared to the locker room. I wanted his mind to be in a good place, even if I had to sell him a falsehood for the time being. I would be sure to enlighten him after the game.

Just because I understood his mom's mental state didn't mean I agreed with it, nor would I ignore it for long. Ignoring the toxic behavior was enabling it. Because she was older than me, she looked at my calling out her behavior as disrespectful. She probably viewed Nate's response to it as disrespectful as well.

I slid on my black leather-like leggings, a black, white, and blue halter top, and blue heels. I thought I would show Nate that I was repping his team colors. Once I applied my makeup and twisted my dreads just how I liked them, there was ten minutes to spare. I surely didn't want to go downstairs a minute too soon. It was bad enough we would have to travel there together.

I began cleaning up my mess and made Nate's bed. By the time that was done, it was definitely time to get to the car. I grabbed my blue blinged-out clutch and blue sweater and headed down. I could see Ms. Green making her way to the door as I did so. The minute I walked out of the door, she went in. "I was wondering if you were going to make the game."

I slightly rolled my eyes then got in the car. She got in next to me. "I suppose your lil stunt didn't work."

"Although he got irritated, he knew why I said those things. He assured me that my place in his life is secure. You may need to inquire about yours. However, I refused to go into detail about your words of venom before his game. His mind needs to be on playing to the best of his abilities tonight, especially since he's missed a few games."

She turned her head away from me, thankfully, so I did the same. I looked out the window at the passing scenery. I had only been to Dallas a couple of times before now. There was a lot of land, nothing like Chicago. Everything seemed so jam packed compared to here. I kind of liked this. It just seemed peaceful. While I knew there were urban areas in Dallas, it didn't make up the entire city.

Ms. Green was way too quiet, and it somewhat made me nervous. She was sitting there in her head and there was no telling what was floating around in there. When I looked over at her, my heart softened somewhat. She looked sad and at the point of tears. Maybe she was reevaluating her place in Nate's life as I suggested.

"Ms. Green, there is enough room in Nate's life for the both of us. I understand your closeness. My mother and I are very close. Any man that can't accept that couldn't be in my life. I'm not trying to take your place. I'm trying to fill another position. You're his mother."

She turned to me, and I noticed her lip trembling. This was resolving a lot quicker than I anticipated. "Although my parents are alive, it has always been Nate and me. Wherever I went, Nate was with me. If he couldn't tag along, it was rare that I went, except work, of course. I sacrificed everything to assure he had a good life."

"I know he appreciates that," I said as I reached for her hand.

She grabbed it, and I could feel the tremble coursing through her. "I'm sorry. I just… I don't even know how to explain it. He's my baby. It was hard when he left to play ball overseas. I wanted him to be successful. I've always wanted the best for him. But... I just want to always be a part of it. It's like I'm scared to live without him."

"You are extremely attached to him, but, Ms. Green, you have to live your life for you now. Nate is a grown man. I know you want grandbabies to spoil. I *do* want kids one day. Yes, I'm getting older... I'm nearly forty, but it's not too late. So let us move at our pace. We aren't forcing it. It's organically moving at this speed. I know it's unbelievable for you, because it's unbelievable for me."

She nodded. "Please don't hurt my baby. I can see that look of admiration in his eyes whenever he looks at you. He's already falling."

I smiled slightly. "I won't hurt him. He's a good man. I can feel his love every time he stares at me. My entire body heats up under his gaze. The last thing I want is to cause a riff between the two of you. Your mother-son relationship is important. Thank you for raising a man that knows how to treat and respect women. He's everything I've ever desired."

She smiled and squeezed my hand. "Thank you for this. Sometimes I feel like I'm losing him. I hate that feeling, and it causes me to behave in unbecoming ways. It makes me feel defensive. I know it will mean a lot to him to see us getting along. So instead of looking at it as I'm losing a son, I suppose I should see myself gaining a daughter."

Her words touched my heart. My iciness was gone. I leaned over and lightly kissed her cheek then gently wiped the bit of lipstick from it as she smiled. "Thank you for being patient with me, Kenya. I owe Nate an apology."

"Come to courtside with me when we get there." Her eyebrows lifted. "It will do him some good to see that we've squashed the issue between us and that we are both here to root him on... together."

She nodded. "Okay. Let's do it."

I silently thanked God this shit was done. I was glad I didn't get too out-of-pocket with her, or this moment probably wouldn't have ever happened. While the devil tried to interfere in our progress, we couldn't let him win. He had to flee. I was beyond grateful that he didn't hang around too long. That only proved to me how this was meant to be. Nate and I would be together no matter what tried to come against us if we kept our eyes on what was the most important: our journey to love.

CHAPTER 17

NATE

I couldn't have been more pissed at my mama. She came to Dallas and did just what the fuck she wanted to do anyway. I was two seconds from putting her out of my house. When Kenya tried to appease her by offering to pay for shit, I knew they'd had words before I got there. When Kenya said that things were fine, I knew she was lying.

I wasn't a stranger to how my mom could be. She was that way with all my girlfriends growing up. However, those relationships were never that serious for it to even matter. That was why I never introduced Jessica to her though. I started having feelings about things with Jessica moving even slower than I anticipated or not lasting at all. My mom had witnessed my heartbreak from that situation though, and, of course, she was wanting to get at her.

She knew that I was really serious about Kenya because of how fast we were moving. She met her at Noah's house and was meeting her again as my woman two days later. That shit sent her into orbit. She was cool in Baltimore because Kenya and I were only flirting and shit. When Kenya had shown up in Houston, though, it blew her fucking mind.

However, when she joined Kenya courtside to give me kisses of good luck, I was shocked. I could see genuine happiness on both their faces. I supposed *they'd* had a come to Jesus meeting on the way to the arena. Seeing them getting along improved my mood tremendously. It was almost like I'd never missed a game.

Kenya informed me that I had twenty-one points, five rebounds, two blocks, and ten assists. Baby girl stayed on my shit. It helped that she loved basketball. I told her as soon as basketball season was over, we would have a game of one-on-one so I could see her skills. She said she'd played in school. I was pretty sure our one-on-one would lead to other things though.

We won that game by ten points, and when I joined her after the game, she informed me that my mom had left so she could get back on the road. I wasn't upset about that. Although they'd made up, she was still in her feelings. Once I was showered and dressed, I called her on our way home. I let her know how proud of her I was for squashing her qualms with Kenya, and for being a great mother.

"Hello?"

"Hey, Ma. I hate you had to leave. We were going to go celebrate the win."

"I know, but I had to get back."

It was a three-and-a-half-hour drive from Dallas to Houston. She probably wouldn't get home until one in the morning. "I understand. Listen. Thank you for accepting Kenya as my woman. I'm falling for her. I feel so strongly for her already. Nothing anyone could say would cause me to let her go. Unless she becomes a trifling individual, I'm gon' ride for her until I die. She means that much to me already."

"I realized that. She didn't go off on me like she could have, but it was something she said that had me reevaluating my actions and what could be the result of them. She said her position in your life was

secure, but mine may not be. Just like you stopped talking to me when it came to your dad, I knew you would stop talking to me when it came to her. She's a good woman, son."

"I know she is. That's why I was willing to ride for her at all costs. That's my baby, Mama. That's the woman I want to build with. She brings me joy, peace, and love. We haven't declared our love for each other, but I can feel that shit whenever I gaze into her eyes. Somebody once said that the eyes were windows to the soul. I found that to be true. It would have killed me to sever our relationship again, but I would have done it without hesitation when it came to that beautiful angel."

"I know. I don't want to lose you just because I can't let go to let you live your life. You're my all, and I was being selfish, not wanting anyone else to find out how great you are. To hell with basketball. I mean how great of a man you've become. You represent all my best qualities. Your dad's too. I made so many mistakes concerning you, baby. I'm grateful that you haven't grown to resent or hate me."

"You mean the world to me and always will. It doesn't matter who else is in my life. You will always be my mama. There will always be a place for you, Ma. I love you."

"I love you too. Enjoy your time with Kenya, and I'll talk to you soon."

We were in Baltimore, getting ready for TAZ's surprise birthday party. I was sure deep down that she knew what was going on. She and Noah had such a tight spiritual connection, there was no way he was flying under the radar with this.

It had been two weeks, and Kenya had become a frequent flyer. She was with me whenever she wasn't in the studio. She was hopping flights at least twice a week. She'd had to record background vocals for Tank and practice with the other background singers for the show with Ledisi in two weeks. Plus, she would soon start recording for *The*

Masked Singer. I was so excited for her. She was really doing her thing without living under TAZ's shadow.

We were in round one of the playoffs, and we were leading the series, two to one. We would be playing game four in Washington D.C. tomorrow. We'd won both of our home games, and they'd clinched a game at their arena last night. If we could just win our home games, we would win the series, but our goal was to steal the game tomorrow night and end this round early.

Kenya was moving around quite a bit, trying to get things prepared while TAZ stayed here with Brooklyn, Noah, and me. She told TAZ she had a few errands to run and had a session she needed to get to the studio for. When TAZ asked why she couldn't use Noah's studio, she told her someone else had booked the time at another studio. That story seemed to suffice.

As I sat, relaxing, the doorbell rang. I assumed it was RJ, because that nigga was always popping up. It was like Noah's home was his second home. As I heard Noah making his way to the door, I texted my baby. *Damn, girl, I miss you already.*

We'd been together for the past couple of days. She met me in D.C. day before yesterday. When I wasn't on the court, I was in her sanctuary. That woman gave me love, and in the total of a month's time of officially being her man, I was in love with her. The past two weeks had been phenomenal. Seeing how much I meant to her to where she was traveling all over the place to be with me was the icing on the moist ass cake.

Whoever was at the door definitely wasn't RJ. I would have heard him by now. I glanced back and saw Noah heading my way with an older gentleman. Out of respect, I stood from my seat as he stared up at me. The tears in his eyes caught me off guard. I frowned slightly, trying to figure out what was going on.

The tears fell down his cheeks as he said, "Hello, Nate. I'm your grandfather, Harold Guillory."

My eyes widened, and I grabbed his extended hand. He pulled me to him as I stood there in shock. I glanced at Noah to see the smile on his face. My grandfather wrapped his arms around me. "My God. You look just like your father."

I could feel my face heating up as I hugged the old man back. The tears were making their way to my eyes, but I fought to keep them from falling. Noah had gotten my grandfather to meet me here since we could never sync our schedules to go to Houston. Once he released me, he pulled away, and we sat. He wiped his face and said, "My wife would have been so happy to meet you. David would have loved you just as much as he loved Noah."

"Or more," Noah added.

I couldn't form words just yet. Had that nigga told me, I would have been better prepared. My grandfather was tall, just like me. I was maybe a couple of inches taller than him. We had the same medium brown complexion and the same thick lips. Looking at him, I could see so much of myself. "It's nice to meet you," I finally got out.

He nodded and smiled. "I uhh… I didn't know I would be meeting you today, so I'm in shock a lil bit. You're the first person, besides Noah, I'm meeting that had a connection to my dad. In a way, I feel like I'm meeting him through you. So thank you for coming."

He closed his eyes briefly and nodded. "When Noah called me and asked me to come for the party, there was no way I would have turned him down. Although we don't get to see each other often, he will always be my grandson. When he said you would be here and had expressed an interest in meeting me, it made my heart swell. I gave your mother a hard time years ago. I couldn't understand why she waited until David died to say something. Once I got past myself and how I felt about you, she'd distanced herself, and I didn't know how to contact her."

I nodded. "I felt a way about that too. Although I was a kid, I couldn't understand why she kept me from him. I think she was hurt that David didn't want to be with her. While it's not a legitimate reason, I believe that was what it was."

"None of that matters at this point. What matters is that we are here now, getting to know one another. Goodness… you remind me so much of David. You look like him, and your voice even sounds like his. You're a lot more mature than he was at your age though." He chuckled. "You're thirty-two, right?"

"Yes, sir. I'll be thirty-three in September."

"I saw you changed your last name to Guillory. I'm happy that you were accepting of the truth and wanted to be a part of his legacy."

"It wasn't like he denied me. He didn't know. I sought out Noah to find out as much about him as possible. I know I'm about to find out even more now."

"Yep. We'll exchange phone numbers, and whenever you come home to Houston, you are more than welcome to come to the house and look at pictures and stuff. I'll make a court-bouillon," he said as he glanced at Noah.

"I'm coming too then!" Noah added.

"You remember what happened last time you ate it, don't you?" Grandpa asked.

"Yeah, but I overdid it. I gotta have a taste. My pops know how to make it, but I haven't had it in years."

"Have a taste of what?"

There was no mistaking RJ's voice. He'd walked in on the conversation as TAZ joined us with Brooklyn. "Oh! Hey, Mr. Guillory! How are you?" RJ said. "Knowing Noah, y'all must be talking about court-bouillon."

"You are absolutely right. How are you, RJ?" he asked as he stood and shook his hand.

"I'm good. Y'all were talking about food, and that caught my attention. So, I missed all the action, huh?"

We all laughed, then Noah introduced TAZ and Brooklyn to him as I stared at my grandfather. I was close to my grandparents on my mama's side growing up, but not so much now. It was like they didn't want me to know my father either. They took my mom's side on everything. I yearned to be close to them again, but it didn't seem they wanted to be. I left well enough alone. So, to have my paternal grandfather sitting here, wanting to know me was somewhat overwhelming.

Finally, my grandfather asked RJ, "What action are you talking about?"

"Y'all two meeting. I already know Nate looked like a deer in headlights. Noah likes surprising people."

I rolled my eyes and chuckled, and so did Grandpa. "Well, he did, somewhat. Had I not known, I would have looked the same way."

"So, umm... do your other grandkids call you Grandpa?"

He nodded. "Yes. That's what they call me. If you're comfortable with it, you can call me that too."

I nodded as I tried to keep the tears at bay. RJ helped when he tried to give me some tissue. Everybody burst into laughter as I playfully pushed him away from me, then snatched the tissue from him. I swore, that nigga didn't miss a thing.

WHEN TAZ WALKED INTO THE VENUE, SHE LOOKED GENUINELY surprised. We were all standing, singing happy birthday to her. To say it was such short notice, there were quite a few people in attendance— family, friends, and executives. I leaned over to Kenya and said, "She looks beautiful."

"She really does. She thought they were going to dinner."

I smiled. Raqui had picked up Brooklyn and me, telling TAZ that we were going to have fun of our own while she and Noah went to dinner. Since we were playing Washington, she didn't question why I was there. She just assumed I was visiting because I was close by. I just knew she had figured out everything by now.

Grandpa and I had talked so much while he was at the house. I'd invited him to the game tomorrow since he wasn't leaving until the day after, and he said he would be honored. He could see the similarities in the way my dad and I played basketball. I'd also gotten a chance to reach out to Brixton, Jessica's fiancé. I could tell he was somewhat on edge when I called, probably because he didn't know what I wanted.

I assured him that this conversation would be on the up and up. I also assured him that I wouldn't disrespect him in no way, which was the reason for my call. He obviously knew I had talked to either Lennox or Jakari to even have his number. Once he was relaxed, he gave me his blessing to speak to her privately.

I glanced over to where they were seated and admired their beautiful princess. I was pretty sure that baby had set shit off on that plane. Before I could look away, her eyes met mine, and she gave me a slight smile. Jessica Monroe was a beautiful woman, but thankfully, I didn't feel like I was about to lose my shit because of her presence. I knew that had everything to do with the woman standing next to me.

I pulled her closer to me, and she lifted her head and puckered her lips. I kissed her tenderly, slightly pulling her bottom lip into my mouth. This woman had me gone, and I was prepared to let her know tonight after everything was done. I couldn't wait to make love to her. She'd been running all day, so we didn't get to spend much time together.

As Noah led TAZ to her chair, the birthday song by Destiny's Child started to play. TAZ was smiling big and waving at people. Noah went to the mic and said, "Just so y'all know, this is going to be real informal. We here to have a good time, celebrating the woman that has brought so much to the industry and to my life. My love for her is without bounds. Happy birthday, baby. I hope you enjoy tonight."

She blew him a kiss, then he said, "So the servers will be serving your dinner, and while that is going on, we will get entertained by Rachelle Ferrell!"

The crowd applauded loudly. I wasn't that knowledgeable about who she was, but Kenya definitely was. She stood to her feet and applauded, along with TAZ. The singer wished TAZ a happy birthday and said a few more kind words to her, then began singing. The woman was a beast with it. I could see why TAZ and Kenya loved her.

When the woman set the chicken fettuccini alfredo in front of me, I licked my lips. That shit looked so damn good. I forgot all about Rachelle up there and began stuffing my face. Raqui and I had taken Brooklyn to Chick-fil-A, but those lil ass nuggets didn't stay with me long. When Kenya sat down, I was nearly finished. She frowned slightly, then said, "Damn. I guess you were hungry."

"Hell yeah. You know I like to eat," I said then bit my bottom lip, mentally taking her exactly where I wanted her to go.

She squirmed in her seat as I chuckled. She gently shoulder bumped me. "Don't tease me, Nate. I'll have you digging me out in one of these storage closets."

"Shiiiid, you ain't said nothing but a thang, girl."

She giggled then started on her food. My nerves were starting to heighten because I knew now was the time to try to talk to Jess. I noticed her mother had the baby, and she was done eating. However, I didn't want to approach her without Kenya standing next to me. I wanted her to see the love I found with the woman that was meant for me.

"Kenya, I want you to come with me to approach Jess. I need her to see the chemistry between the two of us so she'll know it isn't put on."

I almost said so Jess would see the love I had for her. This was not how I wanted to tell her I was in love with her. I wanted it to be more romantic and in an intimate setting. Cameras were flashing every-where. "Okay. I'm almost done."

I nodded as I felt a tap on my shoulder. I turned to see Jakari,

Yendi, Lennox, and Nesha. Yendi was a beautiful pregnant woman. I slapped Jakari's hand, then Lennox's. After giving the ladies hugs, I said, "What's up, y'all? How y'all been out there in Big City Nome?"

Yendi giggled. That was what they called their lil ass town of four hundred fifty people. "'Bout time you put some respect on Nome, nigga!" Jakari said. "Everybody good. The mayor actually doing his damn job, business is good, and the population is growing, thanks to Nesha's village and us having all these kids."

I laughed then turned to Kenya. I grabbed her hand and helped her from her seat. "Y'all, this is my lady, Kenya Zenith. Kenya, this is Jakari. You spoke to him through text when I had that concussion. That's his fiancée, Yendi."

She hugged them both, then I introduced her to Lennox and Nesha, letting her know how Lennox was my mentor my first year at Lamar when I was running track. I also let her know he kicked me to the damn curb after he got married. He laughed about that and promised we'd link up soon.

"Now baby, this is the Henderson family. These four are only a small fraction of how deep they run. I promise, nearly the entire population of Nome is related to them. All the businesses belong to them. So, although they're acting modest, they are really a big deal."

Surprising me, she asked, "So y'all are related to Jessica? How are y'all adjusting to her career? She's blowing up, right?"

Jakari rolled his eyes. "She got the big head, but that ain't nothing new. She still the same old Jess to us."

Nesha pushed him as Kenya smiled up at me and wrapped her arm around mine. "I'm ready if you are, baby."

"Y'all, come on. I'm going to y'all area."

Jakari nodded as Nesha's eyes widened somewhat. Lennox leaned in and asked, "What are you doing?"

"Don't worry. Brixton knows. Everything's cool."

"If you say so."

As we headed that way, I could feel Kenya tense up a bit. I leaned over and said, "They're all nice, except Storm. Just ignore his ass if he gets out of pocket."

"Which one is Storm?"

"The one looking at us with a frown on his face."

She giggled. "Okay."

When we approached, I could see the nerves crawling all over Jess as she rocked the baby. I supposed her mom had given the baby back to her while I talked to Jakari and Lennox. "What's up, everybody?" I said loudly.

Everyone waved back, and a few of them came over and shook my hand. Brixton stood and extended his hand to me. We shook, and I introduced him to Kenya. He nodded, and she did as well, then I introduced Kenya to Jess. "Kenya, this is Jessica. Jessica, this is my lady, Kenya."

Jess stood with the baby and gave us a huge ass smile. She gave Kenya a half hug as Kenya went crazy over the baby. "Go ahead, man," Brixton said. "Kenya can sit with us and hold the baby."

Kenya's eyebrows hiked up, probably because she was excited to hold the baby, as Jessica frowned. Brix took the baby from Jess, and I grabbed her hand, leading her away from them. "Better not be no fucking funny business though."

I already knew that was Storm. There was a bunch of people shushing him as Jessica chuckled. The tremble in her hand let me know she was nervous about what was about to happen. Once we got to the foyer of the venue, I led her to a bench. Once she sat, I sat next to her, still holding her hand in mine. I angled my body to hers, and said, "I know you're probably wondering what's going on."

"Yeah. Obviously, Brix knows."

"Yeah. I got his number from Jakari to ask his permission to speak to you privately."

She brought her other hand to mine. "I saw the clip on Sports-

Center where the reporter asked if you were dating Kenya. I could see the love in your eyes when you responded."

"Stop feeling guilty about what happened between us. I'm a grown ass man. I fell in love with you, but you weren't the woman meant for me. I can see that now, because what Kenya and I have feels totally different. You're a beautiful woman, and you have a kind heart. Brixton is a blessed man. Let go of the shit you carrying so you can enjoy your life with him and that beautiful baby."

The single tear fell down her cheek, so I gently wiped it away. She'd been trying to hold her emotions in since we sat. I could see it in her tensed shoulders and quiet demeanor. She lifted her head and said, "Nate, you are so perfect. Now that you have Kenya, I know y'all are perfect for each other. I felt so damn bad about hurting you. I'm not a heartbreaker. I led you on to believe we would have more, then chose someone else. That wasn't right."

"It wasn't, but I'm cool now, girl. You ain't gotta act all nervous around me now. You got your one, and I have mine. Brix is the man that moved your soul, so that's who you should be with. Had you chosen me, that shit wouldn't have worked out, because I felt stronger for you than you felt for me. You would have been miserable. So, when is the wedding?"

She smiled and wiped the tear that fell. "I don't think I would have been miserable, Nate. I had strong feelings for you as well." She took a deep breath and continued. "Well, you know we're utilizing the family barn. That shit gon' be so beautiful. We're getting married in September. So, I can send you an invite?"

"Hell yeah. Me and Kenya would love to come and turn up with y'all Henderson style."

I stood from the bench and helped her to her feet as well. Leaning over, I kissed her forehead. "Thanks, Jess, for caring about me. I'll never forget that."

"Thank you for loving me, Nate. I'll never forget that either." She grabbed my hand and said, "Let's go see what they are up to. I heard the music kick up."

I smiled at her and allowed her to lead me back inside. When we walked in, I hollered with laughter. Kenya was dancing with Storm. "I'll be damned if she ain't got Uncle Mayor on the dance floor! She is definitely special, Nate."

I slowly shook my head as Jess made her way back to Brixton with a smile on her face. While I still felt something for Jess, it was nowhere near what I was feeling for Kenya. Tonight had proven that I was completely open and ready to be in love and truly move on in life with Kenya by my side.

CHAPTER 18

KENYA

"So should I call you Uncle Mayor? I heard your niece say that. Y'all feel like family to me because of how cool y'all are with Nate."

"See, you and Yendi smart as hell. Y'all know how to butter a nigga biscuit. These muthafuckas around here disrespectful as fuck. I done got in office and made Nome great again, and they don't appreciate that shit."

I stood there in front of him with my eyebrows slightly lifted, until his brother, introduced to me as Jasper, pushed him and said, "Nigga, shut the fuck up. Can't take yo' ass no-damn-where. Can take the nigga out the country, but can't take the country out the nigga."

"Jasper, carry yo' ass on. I'm talking to Kenya."

I giggled then leaned over to grab his hand. I had to lay it on thick. Since Nate said he was the mean one, I knew if I got on his good side, I wouldn't have shit to worry about. "Uncle Mayor, if it's okay with your wife, you wanna come dance with me? I recognize your greatness. Leave them people in your dust."

His wife rolled her eyes as he stood and glanced at her. "It's okay with her. Come on here, girl. Nate alright with me, with his tall ass."

I chuckled as we got to the dance floor next to Noah and TAZ and danced to "Slow Dancing" by Kenyon Dixon. Regardless of the song title, it was more of a mid-tempo cut. Uncle Storm had rhythm. I liked him already. He grabbed my hand and spun me around as I laughed. He was tall, too, despite him talking about Nate. Maybe only a couple of inches shorter. It seemed most of the men in their family were tall.

I glanced toward the foyer, trying to see when Nate and Jess would make their way back inside. Although I knew he wouldn't do anything to jeopardize us, I was still a little on edge. I supposed Uncle Mayor could sense it. "His sensitive ass ain't out there doing nothing but talking. I was just fucking with them when they left out. Ain't neither one of them crazy enough to do shit. Brixton will air this place the fuck out, and I would help him."

"I swear I like you. Cool as a damn fan in the window during the summertime."

He frowned slightly, then laughed. "Shiiid, you good people. TAZ is too nice and quiet. You more my speed. Since Nate and Brix cool now, maybe y'all will come to the country and visit."

His twang was a little stronger than Nate's, but it had some hood to it. I loved that shit. As we continued to dance, I saw Nate standing there watching us with a smile on his face. Jess was frowning as she approached us. "Uncle Mayor? You dancing and shit? Who making sure the rest of these niggas doing what they supposed to do?"

"Damn, Jess. I have an assistant. What you think Marcus for? Cut a nigga some slack."

She dropped the act and laughed then grabbed my hand and gave it a squeeze. Somehow, I felt like I knew what that meant. I knew I had a good man. She didn't have to assure me of that shit. Storm grabbed my hand and twirled me again, then said, "I'ma go chill out before they think it's open season to do what they want. When the cat's away, the mice will play."

I laughed, and he did too. "It was nice meeting you, Kenya."

"Same here."

I made my way to Nate as he slapped Storm's hand. When I got to him, he pulled me close. "If you had that affect on that nigga, I know for sure you're an angel."

I giggled. "So, I assume the conversation went well."

"Yeah. She saw what I'd said when a reporter asked me about you. He'd asked if you were my new love interest, and I'd told him yeah. So she was very receptive to what I had to say, believing it was true and not just me trying to make her feel better about what happened between us."

"That's good, baby. I'm glad it went well. She seems nice."

"Shiiiid, don't get on her bad side though."

As I laughed, Noah went to the mic. "So y'all done ate, got entertained by Rachelle Ferrell, cut a lil rug, and now my sister-in-law, Kenya, is about to bless us with her vocals. Y'all get ready!"

Nate's eyes widened. I puckered for him to kiss me then headed to the front. Noah passed the mic to me. "TAZ, you have always been a big sister I could look up to. You taught me about music and even gave me vocal lessons. Everything you learned, you passed down to me. I appreciate those lessons. Now I'm going to sing one of your favorites."

I winked at her, then smiled at Nate as the track was cued up. When I began singing "In The Morning" by Ledisi, TAZ stood to her feet. "Kenya, you better sang!" she yelled.

I nearly laughed in the mic. When we were younger, I used to imitate Ledisi a lot, so I could mimic her well. I did every run she did and even did the growls. TAZ took off her shoe and threw it toward me, causing the crowd to laugh. However, when I brought my attention to Nate, he seemed to be in awe. Not many people had heard me sing this way. It was rare I sang by myself in front of a crowd.

His lips were parted and everything. When I sang, *I need you here with me,* the most challenging part of the song for me, transitioning from the bridge back to the chorus, I stared right at him. My eyebrows were lifted, and my facial expression probably looked horrible trying to hit those high notes full voice, but I didn't care. I wanted him to know how much I needed him. I wanted him to know how much I loved him.

I'd never fallen so fast for anyone. The crowd erupted as TAZ threw her other shoe. She had Brooklyn trying to take off her shoes to throw. Once I ended the song, it was like Nate's gaze had pinned me to that very spot. Noah approached me and took the mic, then said, "Bruh, come get your woman. Excuse my language, but she tore this the fuck up! Kenya, yo' ass been holding out on me. That's okay. I got something for you, girl."

I closed my eyes and graciously bowed my head as the crowd applauded, giving me a standing ovation. Nate walked over to me and grabbed my hand, backpedaling away from Noah. Suddenly, I heard RJ's thunderous voice say, "Hell naw. Y'all need to leave with that shit. I can tell this ain't finna be kid friendly."

As if his and Noah's language was kid friendly. Nate slowly shook his head and pulled me to him. He picked me up, cradling me to him like no one else was in the place. The crowd roared as he carried me right out of there. When we got to the foyer, he finally said, "Shit. I'm in awe of you, Kenya. I had no idea you could sing like that."

"No one knew. Just TAZ and my mama."

"Well, you better get ready. The world about to know. Is that something you want?"

"I don't know."

"I can guarantee it's already online."

"Why? Because you put it there?"

"Hell yeah. I had to brag on my baby. I was live. I propped my phone on the table and let it do what it do. At one point, nearly twenty thousand people had hopped on. There was no mistaking who you were, because I said multiple times, 'my baby killing this shit' and 'sing, Kenya'. That was amazing."

"Thank you, Nate."

"Were you singing that to me? That 'I need you here with me' part? You wanna wake up to me every morning?"

"When possible, yes. Nate, there's so much I want to share with you."

He put his finger over my lips. "I have a lot to say to you too, but we gon' wait until we get to the hotel room. Okay?"

I nodded. At that moment, I knew we wanted to say the same things to each other. I loved Nate, and I knew that he loved me too. I couldn't wait to hear the words fall from his lips.

When we walked back inside, we nearly ran right into my mama and Brooklyn. They were probably going to the restroom. She hugged me tightly then pulled away and put her hand to my cheek. "That's my girl. You showed them what I always knew you could do. Damn. You sang the hell out of that song, my girl. I'm proud of you."

"Thanks, Mama."

I kissed her cheek then bent over to kiss Brooklyn and allowed Nate to lead me back inside. When we walked in, nearly five people approached me all at once. They all chuckled, then allowed one to speak first. He was from Sony Music. They had to be crazy if they thought I would consider signing with anyone other than Noah's label, You Know My Name.

"No disrespect, sir. I'm with YKMN records."

"I should have known better. Good luck to you. You have an amazing voice."

"Thank you."

When he walked away, the rest of them did as well. Before we could sit, Uncle Storm approached us. "Nate, yo' ass better be glad I'm married already. A voice like that? I would have snatched her ass up."

They laughed as he said, "Naw, I'm just kidding. Amazing job, Kenya."

"Thanks, Uncle Mayor."

I kissed his cheek as he smiled, and Nate frowned. When he walked away, Nate asked, "Uncle Mayor?"

"Yeah. That's what Nesha and Yendi called him, so I joined in. I realized they were kissing his ass, and I wanted the clean side of the storm. That dirty side packs all the punch: howling winds and rain. No thank you."

Nate fell out laughing, causing me to laugh too. I couldn't wait to spend the rest of my life with this man.

WE SLOWLY WALKED INTO OUR HOTEL ROOM FOR THE NIGHT. WE LEFT the party before it was over. Nate had to get up early, and I knew he needed rest. We also needed time to make love, because there was no way he was going to go to sleep without breaking me off. I had been so busy we hadn't had a chance to please one another since we'd been in Baltimore.

He laid his jacket over the back of the chair in the room, then turned around to me and slowly slid my dress straps off my shoulders. I purposely wore this dress because it was easy to get out of. It clung to my curves because of the material, but it wasn't as tight as it looked. As he pulled the dress down my body, he stared into my eyes. "I've been waiting all night for this, baby."

"Me too, Nate. Damn."

Once my dress fell to the floor, he picked me up, as he always did, and held me in his arms like I was his precious jewel. "I thank God for you every day. Taking a chance and shooting my shot was the best decision I ever made. Besides, if I wouldn't have, RJ would have thrown the assist."

I gave him a slight smile. "You were nervous to approach me?"

"Not nervous but apprehensive because I knew you were involved with someone. I wasn't trying to set myself up for failure. But damn if you aren't one of the biggest blessings I've ever experienced."

His words would always move me. No matter how many times I'd heard them, my heart only expanded with love for him every time he spoke to me this way. That was one of the things I loved about him. He was so expressive. "Nate, you are my biggest blessing, no doubt about it."

He lowered me to the bed, then began taking off his clothes. His lean but defined body never failed to claim my attention. The man was so damn fine. He licked his lips as he continued to stare at me while he disrobed, and I swore I was about to automatically combust. I slid my hand down my body until my fingertips reached my thong. I eased it to the side and slid my middle finger over my clit.

Staring at him while I did so only made me hotter. He was moving so slowly. I literally wanted to cry and throw a fit if he didn't touch me soon. Slowly sliding my finger over my clit, I then brought it to my mouth, sucking the moisture from it. Nate grabbed his dick and stroked it slowly as he watched me.

"Nate... please..."

"Naw. Keep going, Kenya. Let me watch you please yourself."

I lifted my hips and pulled my thong off and sat up to unfasten my strapless bra. Nate stepped closer to the bed as he licked his lips, but he hadn't stopped stroking his erection. I needed it so bad, but he was teasing me. Lying back, I once again slid my fingers to my pussy and slid one inside, arching my back to receive it like it was a dick.

Before long, I'd added two more fingers, stroking myself slowly, doing my best to entice Nate to put an end to this by sliding his dick inside of me. I moaned while gripping my nipple with my other hand. When I withdrew my fingers and began flicking my clit back and forth, I closed my eyes, trying to imagine it was Nate's tongue.

I didn't have to imagine long, though, because he whispered against my hand, "I'm just torturing both of us. Let me get at my pussy, baby."

I moved my hand, and he slowly pulled my clit into his warm mouth. I grabbed the hair atop his head and held on for dear life. I knew it wouldn't take long, because I was way too turned on. Instead of him getting me to this point, I was already there when he started. Within seconds, I was releasing a waterfall and bucking against his face.

"Fuck, Nate! Oh my God, baby!"

He gripped my hips and pulled me to him, slightly lifting my hips from the bed as he devoured every centimeter of my shit. Without warning, he dropped me back to the bed and entered me with haste. "Kenya, fuck! I don't know how you did this shit so fast."

"It was you. How did... you do it?"

He stroked me slowly as he stared into my eyes. His gaze pulled the tears from my eyes. This moment was more intense than I'd ever felt between us. I knew our love for one another was on full display, and it was ruling our love making. Staring into his eyes, I said, "You are more... than I ever thought you would be. More... than I could have ever imagined."

"Mmmm... fuck," he said as he his eyes closed briefly.

His strokes became stronger, literally lifting me from the bed. I wrapped my legs around his waist and my arms around neck, sinking my teeth into his shoulder. "Girl, you my everything. The way I feel for you is new for me. It's deeper than I've ever felt for anybody. Kenya, fuck... Kenya, shit!"

His body trembled as he fed me his love in every stroke, promising to take me places unseen. After gently biting my nipple and allowing his saliva to fall from his mouth to it, he sucked it into his mouth, bringing me to orgasmic pleasure once again. "Oh shiiiit! Naaaate!"

Just as my orgasm was dying down, he thrusted into me one last time and released his seed all over my cervix. "I love you, baby. Fuck! I love you, Kenya."

"I love you so much, Nate... with all that's in me."

Without pulling out of me, he rolled over, landing me on top of him. He began stroking me again from below, making me want to pull my fucking dreads out. I couldn't believe we were in this place so soon. This was a fucking whirlwind love affair. Now that he'd finished inside of me, I knew he would never pull out again. After a month's time, I was okay with that. This shit was crazy, mind blowing, soul stirring, explosive, and totally unbelievable.

I was living in my own fantasy. This happily ever after wasn't a fairytale, but it was just as magical as one. I swore we had lifted from the bed, caught up in our love. Levitation was very possible with as deep as we were into the moment. "I love you, Kenya. I've known for at least a week now. I just didn't know when I would tell you. After that song... I knew without a doubt that tonight would be the night I gave you everything I'd been holding inside."

"It feels amazing to have love reciprocated. To know you feel as strongly for me as I feel for you touches me deeply. After being in a relationship where the other person didn't value me until I was no longer there, this seems unreal. It's like you are my gift from God for what I endured with Arik. Because of him wasting my time and not being what I needed, it helped me to focus even more on what I *did* need. You are a breath of fresh air, baby. I love you... my one."

I completely relaxed my body on top of his as he continued to make sweet love to me, catering to my body's every need and more. After we both orgasmed again, we fell asleep in that very same position. If things continued to progress the way they were, by this time next year, I would be saying or have already said I do. Besides, love didn't operate by time restraints. I was just thankful we were both willing to act on what we felt, no matter how short a time it had been.

EPILOGUE

NATE

TWO MONTHS LATER...

"And the MVP of the NBA Finals honor goes to Nate Guillory!"

I smiled hard as I accepted the trophy. We'd won the finals for the first time in over ten years. My teammate, LeClaren, threw his arm around my shoulders. "No one deserves this more than you, man. Nobody!"

I lifted it in the air as the cameras flashed. When I stepped off the podium, I went to my baby and hugged her tightly. "I'm so proud of you, Nate! Congratulations, baby!"

I couldn't stop smiling. My entire family was here, celebrating with us, including Grandpa. He and I had established a really close relationship. I'd gotten to meet my aunt and my cousins. Surprisingly, there was no issue with my mama about it. I believed that her issues with Kenya prepared her for this. She still came to most of my games, but she stopped dropping by my house unannounced. That was a good thing, because more often than not, Kenya was there with me, taking all the dick I had to offer.

Her show with Ledisi was a huge success. Ledisi had caught wind of how she tore that song to shreds and invited her to sing it with her. I was standing nearly the entire time, rooting my baby on. Kenya had chosen not to focus on a solo career. She said she would be good with doing features and background singing. Being in the spotlight wasn't her thing. I could understand that. I wanted to be sure that her decision had nothing to do with me, and she tried to assure me, it didn't.

I didn't believe her though. She absolutely loved spending time with me, and I loved every minute of it. A solo career would be extremely demanding. Had this opportunity presented itself when she was younger or even single, I believed she would have hopped all over it. She wasn't hurting for money, so it would be all about the love she had for what she does.

The attorney they'd hired regarding her father's estate and royalties sued the record label, and they ended up paying them millions in back royalties, interest, and fees. There was no evidence found about the speculated homicide claim, so they had to let that go. Kenya, TAZ, and Mama Eunice were so emotional during the proceedings. I was surprised they had even gone to court as quickly as they had.

I lifted Kenya in my arms and spun her around then lowered her. She was so excited. "Thank you, baby."

I kissed her lips, allowing it to linger while the cameras flashed. Our relationship was always in the news for some reason. It was never any bad publicity, but I supposed people liked something they could look up to or draw inspiration or motivation from, like they did Russell Wilson and Ciara. I often saw our picture with the hashtag 'relationship goals'. I thought that was funny, because we had only been a couple for three months.

After celebrating with my team on the court and in the locker room and doing interviews, I showered and went out to find my family still outside waiting for me. I went to my mama and hugged her tightly. "Thank you for all your hard work, helping me get to this point, Ma. You are an excellent mother, and I wouldn't trade you for the world."

"Even with the mistakes?"

"Didn't you learn from them?"

She smiled at me then pulled my head to her to kiss my cheek. "You were a joy to raise, and you've made me proud in more ways than one. I love you, and congratulations, baby."

After slapping Noah's and RJ's hands, I hugged TAZ, Brooklyn, Grandpa, and Mama Eunice. Everyone was so excited for me. Kenya came to my arms and said, "I'm so proud of you! Let's go home and turn up!"

I chuckled as we made our way to the car waiting for us. Kenya was right by calling it home. Wherever I lived was where she lived. When the lease ended on her place, she let it go and moved her furniture into storage. Most of her clothes were divided between my Dallas and Houston houses, since those were the two we would spend the most time at. RJ's architectural firm in Houston had done some remodeling on my house there, and they'd also built us a house in Baltimore. They were fast as hell. That house was done in a month's time.

With Noah and TAZ being there, I knew it would benefit us. While we weren't there, Ms. Eunice kept everything up since she'd moved out there. She said there was no sense in her staying in Chicago by herself. She'd gotten transferred to the dialysis clinic there, and her name had moved up on the donor's list. Hopefully, before long, she would be getting a new kidney.

Once we got to my house and I saw all the cars, I frowned. "Kenya…"

She smiled as she put her fingers over my lips. "Don't worry. We're about to turn up, remember?"

She hopped out of the car before I could say a word. Everyone had beaten us here, but there were way more cars than there should have been. When I caught up to her, she was opening the back door. I walked in behind her, and the place went up! That was when I realized the Hendersons had filled my place to capacity and had cooked and everything.

The smile that graced my lips couldn't be any bigger. Apparently, Kenya loved their asses as much as I did. Lennox and Jakari were the first ones to congratulate me. "Were y'all at the game?"

"Hell yeah! Nigga, you went the fuck off!" Jakari said excitedly. "Forty points, nigga?"

I chuckled. "I wasn't trying to go to a game six. We needed to wrap that shit up at home."

"That's what's up!"

I made my rounds, giving hugs and handshakes to all the Hendersons and to my aunt Natalie, my dad's sister. Everyone had shown up and shown out for me, even my maternal grandparents. To say I was such a loner a short while ago, I had a huge family now. I glanced at Jess and Brix, and she smiled big as I made my way to them. "Thanks for being here, y'all. I appreciate it, Brix."

"Of course, man. You will always have my respect."

We shook hands, and Jess hugged me, congratulating me. The music cranked up, and when I saw Storm snatch Kenya to dance, I couldn't help but laugh. I supposed that would be their thing whenever they were around each other. I stood there and watched them dance, openly admiring the woman that I loved.

When they were done, she made her way to me and took my hat and put it on her head. "This is so amazing."

"It is, baby. I'm glad to be sharing this moment with you. Thank you for this."

"Y'all want some champagne?" Jakari's mother asked as she stood next to us with a tray.

"Yes, ma'am. Thank you."

I grabbed two glasses and gave one to Kenya. "To the woman I'm gonna spend the rest of my life with. Without you, this shit wouldn't be half as meaningful. Whenever you ready to go to the next level, let me know. I would have married you a month ago."

She smiled as I gulped my drink. I frowned slightly, because she was still standing there with hers. "You didn't let me say what I wanted to say, baby."

"Oh, my bad. I mean, I can just get another glass. No big deal."

She chuckled. Once I snagged another one from Mrs. Chrissy, I went back to her. She smiled. "I just want you to know how much I love you and to inform you that we have already gone to the next level in our relationship."

I frowned slightly. "Okay. I'm confused, baby. I mean, I know we've established how seriously in love we are, but we haven't made anything official."

"Oh, but we have. Nate, you already know that you're my one, but the next level I'm speaking of is parenthood. I'm pregnant."

The End

If you did not read the author's note at the beginning, please go back and do so before leaving a review. ☺

FROM THE AUTHOR...

This story was so beautiful. It went nothing like I saw it going. I assumed Nate would be hung up on Jess for almost the entire book, and that Jess would do some questionable shit that would make me not like her. Not so. Nate was so damn perfect. That proves just how fictional this story is. I want to believe he's the most perfect male character I've ever written. However, sometimes we wanna read about what doesn't exist. That's the whole point of fiction. LOL!

He gave me that impression in Jessica's story, *Where Is The Love*, but I figured there was more to him that I hadn't uncovered yet. Then when Jakari's story came and he was always talking about Jess to him, I was like, *aww shit. Reel it in, Nate.* Plus, when he revealed Jessica's involvement, I was hoping she didn't dip back and cheat on Brix. Then I would have had to hear y'all's mouths!

My impression was all wrong. The man resolved issues as quickly as possible, was considerate, kind, and had a soft heart for the women in his life. He reminded me of Noah in a way, without all the toxic back and forth. LOL! Him contacting Brix before talking to Jess was perfect. Because he was so perfect, it left little room for drama… just the situation with his mom. SMH.

I liked Kenya too! She was a no-nonsense type of sister. She was so trusting, wanting to believe that everyone had the same values as she did. I know where she's coming from with that. Her situation with Arik was also resolved quicker than I expected. The twist at the end about her father came out of nowhere. I wasn't expecting that. I thought Arik would just still be on that good bullshit, when he was the one who had messed up.

The chemistry between her and Nate… whew! They moved fast as hell, just like Noah and TAZ. They were two grown people who knew what they wanted. There was no need for procrastination or hesitancy, because they both refused to project past experiences onto each other. If only everyone could be that way. Goodness. It was refreshing. However, we know this isn't life. LOL!

I was so glad RJ and Uncle Mayor came through with a little comedic relief. Nate was always so serious. He was playful at times, but he didn't really garner laughs the way those two nuts did.

I truly hope that you enjoyed this beautiful ride that probably had you feeling all mushy inside. LOL! As always, I gave it my all. Whether you liked it or not, please take the time to leave a review on Amazon and/or Goodreads and wherever else this book is sold.

There's also an amazing playlist on Apple Music and Spotify for this book, under the same title that includes some great R&B tracks to tickle your fancy.

Please keep up with me on Facebook, Instagram, and TikTok (@authormonicawalters), Twitter (@monlwalters), and Clubhouse (@monicawalters). You can also visit my Amazon author page at www.amazon.com/author/monica.walters to view my releases.

Please subscribe to my webpage for updates and sneak peeks of upcoming releases! https://authormonicawalters.com.

For live discussions, giveaways, and inside information on upcoming releases, join my Facebook group, Monica's Romantic Sweet Spot at https://bit.ly/2P2l06X.

OTHER TITLES BY MONICA WALTERS

by T. Key) (a spin-off of All I Need is You)

Until I Met You

Marry Me Twice

Last First Kiss (a spin-off of Marry Me Twice)

Nobody Else Gon' Get My Love (A KeyWalt Crossover Novel with Better Than Before by T. Key)

Love Long Overdue (A KeyWalt Crossover Novel with Distant Lover by T. Key) (a spin-off of Nobody Else Gon' Get My Love)

Next Lifetime

Fall Knee-Deep In It

Unwrapping Your Love: The Gift

Who Can I Run To

You're Always on My Mind (a spin-off of Who Can I Run To)

Stuck On You

Full Figured 18 with Treasure Hernandez (Love Won't Let Me Wait)

It's Just a Date: A Billionaire Baby Romance (stand-alone series with C. Monet, Iesha Bree, Kimberly Brown, and Kay Shanee)

You Make Me Feel (a spin-off of Stuck On You) (coming 2/20/24!)

The Sweet Series

Bitter Sweet

Sweet and Sour

Sweeter Than Before

Sweet Revenge

Sweet Surrender

Sweet Temptation

Sweet Misery

Sweet Exhale

Never Enough (A Sweet Series Update)

Sweet Series: Next Generation

Can't Run From Love

Access Denied: Luxury Love

Still: Your Best

Sweet Series: Kai's Reemergence

Beautiful Mistake

Favorite Mistake

Motives and Betrayal Series

Ulterior Motives

Ultimate Betrayal

Ultimatum: #lovemeorleaveme, Part 1

Ultimatum: #lovemeorleaveme, Part 2

Written Between the Pages Series

The Devil Goes to Church Too

The Book of Noah (A KeyWalt Crossover Novel with The Flow of Jah's Heart by T. Key)

The Revelations of Ryan, Jr. (A KeyWalt Crossover Novel with All That Jazz by T. Key)

The Rebirth of Noah

Behind Closed Doors Series

Be Careful What You Wish For

You Just Might Get It

Show Me You Still Want It

The Country Hood Love Stories

8 Seconds to Love

Breaking Barriers to Your Heart

Training My Heart to Love You

The Country Hood Love Stories: The Hendersons

Blindsided by Love

Ignite My Soul

Come and Get Me

In Way Too Deep

You Belong to Me

Found Love in a Rider

Damaged Intentions: The Soul of a Thug

Let Me Ride

Better the Second Time Around

I Wish I Could Be The One

I Wish I Could Be The One 2

Put That on Everything: A Henderson Family Novella

What's It Gonna Be?

Someone Like You (2nd Generation story)

A Country Hood Christmas with the Hendersons (Novella)

Where Is the Love (2nd Generation story)

Don't Walk Away (2nd Generation story)

Healing For My Soul (2nd Generation story)

The Berotte Family Series

Love On Replay

Deeper Than Love

Something You Won't Forget

I'm The Remedy

Love Me Senseless

I Want You Here

Don't Fight The Feeling

When You Dance

I'm All In

Give Me Permission

Force of Nature

Say You Love Me

Where You Should Be

Hard To Love

Made in the USA
Coppell, TX
20 February 2025

46195485R00115